Mary Jane Forbes

Choices
And the Courage to Risk

Murder by Design: Book 3

Todd Book Publications

The last of the Hansville connection.

Love,
Mary Jane Forbes

**CHOICES
AND THE COURAGE TO RISK**

*Copyright © 2012 by Mary Jane Forbes
All rights reserved. No part of this book may be used or reproduced by any means, graphic, electronic, or mechanical, including photocopying recording, taping or by any information storage retrieval system without the written permission of the publisher except in the case of brief quotations embodied in critical articles and reviews.*

This is a work of fiction. All of the characters, names, locations, incidents, organizations, and dialogue in this novel are either the products of the author's imagination or are used fictitiously. The views expressed in this work are solely those of the author.

*ISBN: 978-0-9847948-2-9 (sc)
Printed in the United States of America
Todd Book Publications: 4/2012
Port Orange, Florida*

*Author photo: Ami Ringeisen
Photos: Bigstock*

To five cousins:

Rick, Todd, Kerry, Rob and Molly

*I trust this series of books will bring back
fond memories of the yellow jacket, fishing derbies,
and Sunday breakfasts down over the bank.*

Books by Mary Jane Forbes

FICTION

Murder by Design, Series:
Murder by Design – Book 1
Murder by Design: Labeled in Seattle – Book 2
Murder by Design: Choices, And the Courage to Risk – Book 3

Novel
The Baby Quilt … *a mystery!*

Elizabeth Stitchway, Private Investigator, Series:
The Mailbox – Book 1
Black Magic, An Arabian Stallion – Book 2
The Painter – Book 3

House of Beads Mystery Series:
Murder in the House of Beads – Book 1
Intercept – Book 2
Checkmate – Book 3
Identity Theft – Book 4

Short Stories
Once Upon a Christmas Eve, a Romantic Fairy Tale

NONFICTION
Authors, Self Publish With Style

Visit: www.MaryJaneForbes.com

Choices
And the Courage to Risk

Murder by Design: Book 3

Chapter 1

The April shower became a downpour filling the gutters in downtown Seattle streets with gushing water. Gillianne Wilder burrowed deeper into her trench coat, arms hugging her body, hood covering her red hair as she stepped quickly from the Jeep to the opposite side of the street—a better vantage point of the burned-out store known as the Working Girl shop until the fire two days ago.

Skip Hunter stood by Gilly's side, rain pelting his blue windbreaker. He didn't reach out to her. Didn't touch her arm. She had again closed herself off behind a wall, a wall that few could penetrate, certainly not a man with romantic intentions.

It's was a little after seven Thursday morning and pedestrian traffic was beginning to build in Seattle's shopping district. A steady stream of cars passed down the street, slowing in front of the blackened shop to catch a glimpse of the charred remains from the fire that thankfully was kept from spreading and consuming the whole block. Television reporters and the morning newspapers quoted the fire chief saying that evidence had been obtained indicating the fire was the result of an arsonist.

Gilly stood mute, her eyes scanning the two-story shop, the shop where three months earlier she had signed a deal with the owner to manage the shop. The shop where she was going to launch her designs, her label—Gillianne Wilder Fashions. The shop where she was going to establish her business and her dream of entering the fashion world.

No one had been hurt in the fire. She and her baby, only a month old, and two of her staff had lived in an apartment on the second floor.

The most important thing—they all escaped without injury. But she had a staff of four who looked to her for guidance, who believed in her dream and were waiting for her back at the Wellington mansion.

Philip Wellington, what a Godsend he was. The billionaire, a friend of Skip's and her grandfather's, was watching the television reporters that morning. Seeing Gilly standing in front of her shop as it went up in flames, he had called offering his home to her and her staff. A place to regroup.

"Let's walk around back," Skip said. "See if your car can be driven." Skip Hunter—newspaper reporter, a friend who wanted to be so much more—had responded to her call asking him to bring her back to the scene of the fire so she could get her car.

Gilly's eyes turned to the man who had spoken, eyes that for a moment seemed not to recognize the man.

Skip, however, recognized the blank look and flinched. He had lost her again. She was in another world. A business woman trying to make sense of what had just gone up in smoke and what she was going to do about it. He looked into her blank green eyes, shook his head, sighed. "Come on, let's find your car."

Gilly stepped off the curb, walked behind a car stopped in the middle of the street, the driver gawking up at the windows that were smashed by the firemen. She hesitated in front of the shop, windows boarded up against potential looters. What a joke, she thought. There was nothing left to loot—burned fabric, charred shelves, racks, cases. The front of the shop, nonetheless, was cordoned off with yellow tape, and bright orange cones had been strategically placed to keep pedestrians away from the display windows and cracked glass door.

They found that her car had survived unscathed by the battle of the fire engines, hoses, and ladders except for a thick layer of soot now in jagged, clogged, sticky lines from the rain. Gilly unlocked the car, slid in and turned the key. The engine sprang to life. She looked up at Skip, his hand on the top of the open door. "Thanks. I really appreciate you bringing me down here … so early. I'll be in touch."

Skip closed the door and stepped back so she could back away from the building. He watched as she disappeared out of the alley.

Chapter 2

On the way to the Wellington mansion Gilly stopped at the veterinary clinic to check on Coco, her cat. Coco was a hero! She had warned Gilly of the fire, saving everyone's life. Coco, her fur singed, was responding to the veterinarian's care. Gilly told him her mother would be by in a day or two to take the frightened cat home with her to recuperate.

Back at the mansion, Gilly checked on her baby before meeting with her staff. Gladys, Wellington's maid, had happily taken charge of the infant from the moment Gilly arrived in her bathrobe and green Red Cross slipper socks.

Restrained chitter-chatter stopped as Gilly entered the elegant dining room of Philip Wellington's mansion. Wellington had insisted Gilly, Robyn her baby, and Nicole and Gabby, two members of her staff, all rendered homeless because of the fire, come to his mansion and stay for as long as they desired.

Nicole and Gabby exchanged a quick glance as their boss, but more than that, their friend, entered the room. They had met Gilly when she interned at various fashion houses in Paris. Both French women saw a creative designer who was going to be a force in the fashion world, and when Gilly called with a job offer in Seattle they quickly accepted.

Philip Wellington joined the group, coffee in hand, and sat at the end of the glossy teak dining room table—a table that sat twelve and expanded to twenty. He took in Gilly's demeanor, the way she held her body—straight, calm, determined. He recognized her deportment. It was not unlike his own years ago building his cattle ranch in Montana. Twice he thought he had lost everything only to pull himself up by his bootstraps to rebuild, forge ahead, and ultimately to make his fortune. Yes, he thought, Gillianne Wilder had the stuff to come out of this trying situation all the stronger for the setback. Trial by fire, he thought ironically.

Gilly locked eyes with Wellington as she passed to pour herself a cup of coffee. She pulled strength from his eyes, and then turned to face her staff of four. Besides the two members from Paris, there were Maria, her long time friend and confidant, and Arthur the man who had saved her from falling into an oncoming train and was now the manager of her books, head of the accounting department of one. They waited to hear from the twenty-four year old redhead who seemed to have the bearing of an experienced business woman twice her age.

She walked to the empty chair at the head of table. "Well, on one hand, we were frightened out of our wits but we were not hurt. On the other hand, we lost some used furniture in the loft apartment and the studio, a rack of our designs and items on a shelf. And, all our labor sprucing the place up. But, we managed to grab our laptops as we ran out of the building, and Arthur had squirreled away the accounts and all the paperwork to support his numbers at his home. But above all we have our minds, our hearts, and our fierce determination. We may be homeless but we are not helpless."

Gilly took a sip of coffee, sat a moment, but unable to sit still, stood and paced to the end of the table.

"The landlord lost a section of his building and his tenant Stacy Sinclair. Stacy had planned to retire anyway, which is why she asked us to manage the shop. Stacy lost her inventory and her business in the fire and has no interest in reopening the Working Girl shop. Which means the shop's sales will be cut by more than half because Stacy is not going to replace her stock. We only have Nordstrom's display—no more walk-in traffic at the Working Girl, no display in the window, no sales—nothing of Stacy's inventory was saved. The insurance companies will not payout any money until the Fire Chief and the police, along with the insurance investigators, can ascertain that the landlord or Stacy, or ourselves, had nothing to do with igniting the fire. From what the insurance adjustors have said, we can't expect the funds to be released anywhere from a few days, weeks, or months."

Gilly glanced up at Wellington. "Mr. Wellington, I can't thank you enough for taking us in yesterday, and now I'm going to ask you if we can extend our stay for a month, to rent this dining room and the three bedrooms."

"My dear woman, I will be happy to have you move your operation to whatever rooms you have need of for as long as you desire. And don't let me hear the word rent. The activity you have brought to my home and my staff over the last few hours has given us a new lease on life. I for one am going to enjoy watching you and your staff overcome this setback. I will ask Gladys to have this room cleared of everything but the furniture so you have space to work. I will show you additional rooms you might find usable and Gladys will work out menus as needed. Let's call my home the temporary House of Wilder Fashions."

Gilly's lips formed the first smile she'd displayed in the last forty-eight hours. "Mr. Wellington, your hospitality is accepted but we will settle the matter of compensation later."

"Gillianne, the fun I'm going to have watching you triumph over this temporary adversity will be payment enough."

Gilly cocked her head, one brow raised. "You and I *will* discuss this later."

Gladys bustled in setting a carafe of fresh coffee and a tray of bagels and cream cheese on the buffet. She smiled at the group sitting around the table and left.

"Mr. Wellington—

"Please, everyone, call me Philip. If we're going to be business partners of sorts, I have always insisted my colleagues call each other by their first names. Is that all right with you, Gillianne?"

"Perfect. So, Philip, do you have five card tables, or small tables for desk space, to setup in this room? I think it is important, for the next few days anyway, that my staff and I work out of the same room. We're used to close quarters and, until we get our sea legs, I'd like to keep us together. Do you have pads to put on the dining room table to protect the wood? We do need a surface to cut patterns and muslin, oh, and a white board propped on a couple of chairs?"

"Perkins will see to it. I'll ask him to check with you when you're finished with your meeting to see to it you have whatever you need."

"Thank you. I think you have all of our names but I'll make out a list just the same." Gilly looked over her staff. They were beginning to relax. Nicole's eyes no longer looked frightened. It was a beginning. "You all still have jobs. Nothing has changed as far as your roles in our company. We have to dig in and cultivate more buyers now that we've lost our primary revenue stream."

"How are we going to do that?" Nicole asked. The precocious twenty-eight year old was ready to go. She only wanted to know in which direction Gilly wanted her to march.

Everyone laughed. How wonderful it felt to begin to come to grips with the situation. Sweet Nicole piping up, the first to pierce the gloom and doom with her girlish French accent.

"Gilly, wait." Gabby stood, arms across her chest, head down. "This isn't going to work," she said in a soft voice.

The smiles vanished from their faces. Breathing stopped. Gilly studied Gabby and knew instantly that Gabby was right. Gilly had been looking for an easy way out. Wellington had stepped in giving them a place to sleep, food, and a change of clothes. But it wasn't a workable situation to keep the business going.

Gilly stared at Gabrielle Dupont, thirty-nine, the person with the most business experience in the room except for Wellington.

"It would be hard to meet potential buyers in this mansion, several miles from the heart of the city." Gabby lifted her head, eyes darting around at the faces staring back at her.

Nicole turned to Gilly. "Is there a bus stop out here?" she asked her eyes flashing to Wellington.

He nodded in the negative.

"How am I going to get to the factory, to meet with Vinsenso, check for flaws in the day's production?" Nicole added.

"I don't have a car," Arthur said timidly. "That's why Cindy and I live in the city so we don't have the expense of a car."

Gilly sought Maria's eyes signaling they both understood. Gabby was right. The Wellington mansion was not the answer.

"Okay. Here's what we're going to do." Gilly took a deep breath. "Philip, thank you for your offer and forget what I said a few minutes ago—the tables, moving things around. However, you'll never know how grateful I am, we all are, for taking us in the morning of the fire." Gilly expelled the breath she was holding and then smiled. "Now, I have some calls to make. We will reconvene today at my grandfather's house at two o'clock, in Hansville. A *summit meeting*. It's a beautiful, sunny day and I'm sure we'll figure out our next step after a nice ferry ride across Puget Sound. Maria, can you bring Arthur and Cindy?"

"Of course."

"Arthur, I hope Cindy can join us. I'd like her to be in on our decisions. Gabby, I'll drive you and Nicole. But, we have a couple of stops to make first. Let me make my calls. I should be ready to leave in thirty minutes and bring your laptops. Is everybody onboard?"

They all nodded and started picking up their notes to leave.

Gilly walked up to Philip and threw her arms around him, laying her head on his chest. He in turn gripped her tightly. She smiled at him, a twinkle in her eyes. "I dub you my surrogate father. Do you accept?"

"Yes, my dear. With pleasure. Seems you and your grandfather have become part of my life—the both of you helping in the case of my stolen gold. And, of course, Skip staying on the story."

"You know Skip's almost finished his novel ... the *Exposé of Seattle's Gold Heist* I believe he calls it," Gilly said.

"Oh? I knew he was writing something about it. Nice man—good reporter."

"We'll be back tonight but it will probably be after nine. Please let Gladys know that my mom will feed us today. Okay?"

"Okay. I presume you're taking Robyn with you?"

"Always." She gave him a quick peck on the cheek and then she was gone.

Excitement gripped the group again as they headed for the door. A plan of attack was percolating under Gilly's red locks and they wondered what rabbit she'd pull out of her hat this time. It certainly had to be big one.

Chapter 3

The sun continued to shine reflecting brilliant flickers of light off the waters of Puget Sound. In the back seat of the car, Gabby fed Robyn her first bottle of breast milk as the women chattered non-stop from Seattle to Hansville. Coco was asleep in her cat carrier. Gilly honked her horn twice as she pulled into the driveway of her grandfather's house—the home where she had spent most of her time before she moved to Seattle.

Gilly's mom Anne, and Gramps barreled out of the patio door to help with the baby and her bags full of diapers, sleepers, and little outfits Gladys had not been able to resist when shopping for the infant in her charge. It was the first time Gilly had been to Hansville since Robyn was born and the girls headed to her bedroom closet to find a change of clothes. Anne scooped Robyn out of Gabby's arms and headed to the crib she had set up in Gramp's bedroom for her naptime. Gramps let Coco out of her carrier in the kitchen. She seemed to perk up now that she was back in her old stomping grounds.

The aroma of fried chicken filled the house along with fresh-baked bread. Maria, Arthur and Cindy arrived within ten minutes and the little house was suddenly a flurry of activity. Maria showed the new arrivals the lay of the land—the guesthouse where she and Gilly had spent long sessions designing and sewing samples. They then strolled outside to the front of the house and the rickety stairs leading to the deck below, and the ladder down to the beach.

At precisely two o'clock, with full stomachs, Gilly called the summit to order in the living room with the wall of picture windows revealing the sparkling waters of the sound.

Everyone sat in fresh jeans and T-shirts—a few perched on chairs, the rest on the floor leaning against the couch, sneakers forming a hub in the middle of the circle. Coco peered out from under the couch. Gilly sat on the raised hearth of the fireplace a fresh cup of coffee on one side, her tote on the other, and a legal-size yellow pad in her lap. She also wore a smile as did Nicole and Gabby. They had accompanied Gilly on her stops and knew what was coming.

"Gabby, Nicole, and I went to see the landlord of what was Stacy's shop. I asked him if he had anything, *anything*, that we might use while the burned out space was being cleaned, repaired, and made suitable for use again."

"And? Come on. Give, girl friend," Maria said. She knew that sly look. The look meant that Gilly had come up with a solution to their predicament. But what?

"Well ... he did. At first he just shook his head, no. He said that the only vacant space he had was spread over the shoe store and the mobile phone center. The two shops to the left of the Working Girl. He said it was just a '*big, old, dirty, barren floor.*' So, I asked if we could see it."

"My God, Gilly, that would be twice the size of our second floor loft area," Arthur said. "Sounds like the space he's talking about must have sat empty for a long time."

"You are so right Arthur ... a looong time. Who would want it? That *big, old, dirty, barren floor?*"

Gilly took a sip of coffee, looked over at her mom sitting on the edge of her chair in the arched doorway of the dining room ... waiting to hear the deal her daughter had made.

"He led us through the shoe shop to the center stairs, like the staircase in the middle of the Working Girl, and up to the loft."

"Honestly, you guys, it was beautiful ... dirty, empty, but beautiful," Nicole said pulling her knees up to her chest, her eyes big as saucers visualizing what she had seen.

"Plumbing? Does it have water? Heat? A bathroom?" Maria asked.

"All of that, and nothing else. Oh, wait, except for banks of florescent lighting fixtures," Gilly said.

"He must want a fortune," Arthur said, glancing at his wife then back to Gilly.

"Hold on a minute, Mr. Money Man," Gilly said. "This is way more space than we need, I told him. And then Gabby, well, Gabby you tell it."

"I stood glancing around ..." Gabby paused as if anticipating a sale, looked out the window, back at the eager faces in front her. "Glancing around, I said that from the looks of it, it must never have been occupied. I think we'd be doing you a favor if we took over *some* of this space." Gabby looked back at Gilly barely able to contain herself.

"I said, if he would let us squat here *rent free*, we would agree to move back to our original space after he had accomplished the cleanup and renovation. At which time, *I continued*, we would once again pay rent but it had to be at the same rate—no increase just because it was new."

Maria sat shaking her head. "I bet you went so far as to say, if he let us *squat* on the *big, old, dirty, barren floor* we would pay for the heat and electricity just to show him our good will?" she said chuckling.

"Well, yes, but only if he arranged to have a cleaning crew in there today and tomorrow so we could move in on Saturday," Gilly said.

"Wait," Arthur said. "What are you guys going to sleep on? And what about tables, a kitchen set up, partitions, a corner for Gabby's clients?"

"Ahh, well ... that is what we have to do tomorrow ... while the landlord has the floors scrubbed, and the brick walls and beamed ceiling washed down. Before catching the ferry we three went to a furniture warehouse in Everett. We had to see if what we were planning was doable. They had *partitions*, tables, desks, chairs, rolled up rugs, kitchen stuff, even beds. No cribs. Have to work on that. And they will deliver Saturday."

"Oh, Gilly, it sounds awfully rough," Arthur said shaking his head.

"You're right, Arthur, it will be rough. But we'll be in business ... well, kinda, better than miles away ... definitely different than the Wellington mansion."

"Arthur, you should have seen the tiny space Gilly and I plus Sheridan, another roommate, shared in Paris," Nicole giggled. "We couldn't turn around without bumping into each other. Just wait until you see what we girls can do. We'll make it work. You'll see."

"Count me in," Cindy said looking at her husband. "I can at least run errands while you set up."

Gilly smiled at Cindy. "Oh, and there's one more thing. I asked Butch, the landlord's name, if he could ask the cleaners to wash the

Working Girl shop windows and floor where we set up our mannequins. Gabby checked and they were still intact—no cracks. He said he thought he could."

"Why?" Arthur asked.

Poor Arthur, Gilly thought. He's never seen four women in action before. "Nicole and Gabby will put up our window displays again. Of course, the ladies will have to be scrubbed, fresh wigs, and Nicole will dress them in samples of our new collection."

"Gilly, that's brilliant," Maria said. We can keep the public informed of the progress, even tease them a little with what's coming—they'll be part of it—a show."

"That's right. Now, one more thing I want to do ... nothing to do with what I've mentioned so far. We're going to sign up for a spot on the runway in September's fashion week ... in New York!"

Chapter 4

Maria moseyed along the Wellington driveway taking note of the spring bulbs pushing through the mulch. The first week of April. She had stepped outside for a breath of fresh air hoping to stir her creative juices. It was Friday morning, and in a few minutes she and Gabby were meeting to brainstorm some killer ideas for the shop's front window displays as renovations began. Next she'd be off to order a sign for the new store front: *Gillianne Wilder Fashions*.

An hour, and two cups of coffee later, Maria and Gabby were ready to show Gilly and Nicole their ideas. The pair was working at the opposite end of the dining room table.

"Come look," Maria called out. "Here are the concepts and possible signage for the windows to lure pedestrians to pause, peek in, see the reconstruction in action."

Gilly and Nicole stood looking over Maria's shoulder. "I love it," Gilly said. "It adds an element of excitement—

"Excitement," Nicole chimed in.

Scooting to the other end, Nicole picked up the papers she and Gilly had been working on. "Here's the layout of the loft—apartment and studio. Any suggestions?" Nicole asked.

Gabby and Maria made a few comments and then Gilly and Nicole left for the furniture warehouse. Anne was taking care of Robyn in Hansville and would bring her back to Gilly Sunday morning after the *barren* loft was set up. At the warehouse the pair began the arduous task of picking out what they needed to make the empty space livable, rather what they could afford being mindful of Arthur's admonition to try to stay within his budget.

Three hours later they huddled in the office with the warehouse manager and added up their selections. Over budget! They eliminated a few items.

"Close enough," Gilly said, putting the calculator back in her tote.

The manager agreed to arrive at the back of their building at one o'clock the next day and that his men would assemble the eight-foot partitions, and position the furniture including a refrigerator, microwave, and small stove. It was also agreed, that if Gillianne Wilder Fashions replaced a rental piece, the warehouse van would pick up what they didn't need twice a month reducing the rental fee appropriately.

Tired but pleased with their selections, Gilly climbed into her car with Nicole and headed to the building to see what the place looked like as the cleaners did their thing. Hearing her cell, Nicole dug it out of Gilly's tote and handed it to her. It was Detective DuBois.

"Gillianne, Edward Churchill's lawyer and the lawyer for the prosecutor on the case are taking Churchill's deposition in an hour. It's been requested that you attend. Can you make it?"

"Sure. Where?"

"Here, at the department. Ask the desk sergeant to call me and I'll take you to the conference room. Spiky, your blackmailing friend, has been making some comments you might find interesting. Of course, he's trying to plead to reduced charges. Skip Hunter will also be attending."

"Oh. Okay. See you in an hour." Gilly handed her phone to Nicole, and let out a sigh. Her heart began racing. Damn, she thought, why the flutters just because I'm going to see Skip again. She had seen him the morning he helped her retrieve her car. There was absolutely no reason seeing him today should bother her.

Nicole saw Gilly's spirit deflate. "Bad news?"

"Not really. Spiky, that guy who stole my designs a couple of years ago—

"The one who started stalking you, sending red satin hearts with a nail through the middle, and later tried to blackmail you to keep the secret of Robyn's father out of the media? That guy? How could I forget? He stalked you in Paris and back here to Seattle." Nicole looked out the car window. "He's a psycho if you ask me."

"That's the one."

"Creepy." Nicole looked back at Gilly. "You thought he started the fire in the shop."

"He's been in jail on blackmail charges, and the detective who arrested him, that was DuBois on the phone, wants me to be present at his deposition. Seems he's trying to make a deal in return for less jail time. DuBois said Skip is going to be there although I'm not sure why. He's not reporting on the story for the newspaper. No one is."

"You like him … Skip I mean not DuBois," Nicole giggled.

"Skip's always seems to be there for me when I'm in trouble."

Chapter 5

The police department conference room was located in the interior of the building—no windows, eight-foot oak conference table dinged up from hard use. Old oak chairs ringed the table as well as extras placed against the wall. A small cart was pulled up to one end of the table on which a recording machine sat to capture what was said by the various participants.

Detective DuBois escorted Gilly into the room. She was the last to arrive before Edward Churchill was brought in. DuBois told her where Churchill would sit and suggested she take a seat on the opposite side of the table so she could watch him, nodding at the empty chair next to Skip.

Skip stood as she entered the room, gave her a quick hug, and the pair sat down along with DuBois and three lawyers—two from the prosecutor's office. A guard escorted Churchill into the room. He was dressed in a new pair of jeans, white T-shirt, and sneakers. His head was shaved and he walked with a decided limp. No cuffs. An armed guard sat behind him.

The State's attorney started the deposition establishing Churchill's name, age, and address. Churchill gave his parent's fifth Avenue condominium in New York City as his address. The attorney then asked Churchill if he knew the young woman sitting at the table.

"Sure, I know her. That's Gillianne Wilder," he answered with a smirk.

Gilly, no expression of acknowledgement, looked straight into his eyes.

The lawyer shuffled through some papers and pulled out a folder. Opening the folder he laid it in front of Edward. "Do you recognize these letters, note cards?"

Edward shuffled through the pages, looking up at Gilly after each one, smirking.

"Yeah, I recognize them."

"Did you send them or have them delivered in some way to Ms. Wilder?"

"Yup. You see I figured she owed me. It was on account of her that I was fired. Had a great job at a fashion house in New York. And then that old man, her grandfather, shot me for no reason. It's because of him that I'm in constant pain. Can barely walk."

"I see. You said you recognized the letters. In the last two you sent, you asked for twenty-thousand dollars or you were going to tell the news media in Paris who fathered her baby. Is that correct?"

"Yeah. As I said, I figured she owed me."

"Mr. Churchill, we found a deposit of twenty-five thousand dollars in a bank account with your name on it. Here is a statement from that account. Is it your account?"

"Yeah. So?"

"Where did this money come from? Ms. Wilder has stated she never sent you any money."

"It came from Mr. Maxime Beaumont." Edward looked at Gilly and chuckled.

Gilly's mind started spinning. Spiky had received money from Maxime? Did he tell Maxime about her baby?

"And why did Mr. Maxime Beaumont send you this money?"

"Oh, well, you see, Monsieur Beaumont didn't want the fact that he had had a bastard child with an American whore—

Gilly jumped to her feet, leaned with both hands on the table, her green eyes sparking. "Edward, you told Maxime about my baby?" she yelled.

"Mr. Churchill, stick to the facts," the lawyer said. "And, Ms. Wilder, please sit down."

"I am *sticking to the facts*," Edward spit out the words looking straight at Gilly. "He was running for the Senate, the French government, and certainly didn't want the paparazzi to get wind of his little bundle in Seattle. I actually asked for a million Euros. The twenty-five thousand was just the down-payment."

Gilly moved to stand again but Skip gently put his hand on her arm. She remained in her seat, her chest heaving with each breath. *So Maxime knows about Robyn. But a down payment? That didn't make sense.*

Gilly looked at Skip then Detective DuBois. From their expressions she could see they had come to the same conclusion she had hearing Edward's story. The detective's words the day of the fire rang in her ears—"Edward Churchill was in a Tacoma jail. He couldn't have set the fire. Someone else is trying to murder you."

Suddenly the conference room door banged open and a trim woman, a senior citizen, strutted in directly to Edward's side.

It was Helen Churchill, Edward's grandmother.

"Edward dear, I came as quickly as I could. You're grandfather is parking the car. Are you all right? They aren't being mean to you are they?"

"Grandmother, how nice." Edward stood, kissed his grandmother on the cheek and sat down under the pressure of the guard's hand on his shoulder.

Edward's lawyer introduced the grandmother to the State's attorney, gave the relationship, and asked that another chair be made available at the table.

"Oh, I'm not staying," Helen said. "I just wanted my grandson to know we are here to support him." Turning to Edward, she said, "Now you remember that your grandfather and I are working very hard for you. So, don't you worry, dear."

Helen nodded to Edward's lawyer and turned to leave. "Gillianne, I hold you responsible for putting my grandson in this awful situation. If it hadn't been for you, he would still be a designer in New York City. Well, you have seen the last of my money. Why I ever offered to help with your move to Seattle I'll never know. I'm shocked that you kept any of it. I expect to be repaid … with interest. Here I was trying to help you get established and this is the thanks I get … my dear Edward in prison. The very idea that Edward was under suspicion for setting the fire just makes my blood boil." The door slammed shut behind her.

Chapter 6

Paris

The votes were cast. The votes were tallied. Maxime Beaumont was one of several men to win a Senate seat in the French government. His father, Count Beaumont, couldn't stop smiling, his mother was quietly proud of her son. His wife, Bernadette, went on a spending spree. After all, she had to dress the part of a Senator's wife and certainly couldn't be expected to wear let alone be seen in her old wardrobe.

Underneath the gaiety—the new work in the Senate and never-ending social engagements—the Beaumonts, each from their own perspective, fretted.

The Count couldn't decide if he should call off the demise of the American harlot, Gillianne Wilder. The blackmailing of his son had come to an abrupt end. His detective said the blackmailer had been arrested in Tacoma, Washington. One thing the Count was sure of, the result of his son's infidelity producing a bastard child had not come to light during the campaign.

Then there was Bernadette Beaumont, thirty-four, now a Senator's wife added to her status and power. Power because she had agreed to reconcile with Maxime so he could present himself as a steady, happily married man, and thus one who could be trusted by the electorate. Well, married, anyway. But Bernadette, while achieving one goal with the successful election of her husband, still desired to seal her position in the family and partake of their wealth forever. A baby would cement her place. But she and Maxime never conceived a baby in the first year of their marriage, and she had banned him from their bedroom.

Overhearing a heated argument between her husband and his father, she learned her husband had fathered a child. Maybe she had been a bit hasty in her conclusion that Maxime was impotent. But there *was* a baby out there with Beaumont blood running through its little veins. So, Bernadette with knowledge of a baby and learning the identity of the mother from the shouting on the other side of the door, had discreetly hired a detective in Seattle. She wanted to know when the birth was announced. And learn she did—it was a girl!

Bernadette preferred it to have been a boy, but the mere fact the baby existed was good enough, especially since she knew the secret of its birth. How wonderful, she thought. I don't even have to go through the painful, messy process of bearing the child myself. Without a baby the Beaumont blood line ceases with Maxime. Maybe I should continue to employee that detective. Someone to keep tabs on the little treasure, and someone to figure out the best way to bring the little darling to me. Oh, I can just see their faces when I walk in and present Maxime and his father with the baby.

His baby.

Our baby.

Bernadette, one year senior to her husband and to her she was much wiser, had to determine what was in her best interest—bring that baby to the Beaumonts, or be content with her new role as the wife of a Senator.

Pouring a snifter of cognac, twirling the amber liquid in the glass, she developed a course of action. "I have to see the infant first. Then I will decide," she whispered emptying the glass, the contents slowly warming her body as it slithered down her throat.

Maxime, thirty-three, threw himself into his new position as Senator in the French Parliament. He forced himself to concentrate on his new duties, indeed, his new life—one his father had coveted for him since he was born. Maxime always believed that what he was groomed to be—a lawyer and then a senator—was what he wanted as well. But, he found if he wasn't careful his mind wandered to the image of Gillianne. She took over his thoughts. Swimming in his apartment building's heated pool, he decided on four more laps to clear his head.

Unsuccessful, he pulled his six-foot-one body onto the side of the pool. Picking up the towel lying beside him, he dried his short black hair then got to his feet toweling off his muscular frame.

Gazing down at the water with his dark brown, almost black eyes, he ruminated what he learned through his father's detective. Gillianne had given birth to a baby girl—a tiny baby girl with red hair and black button eyes he was told. He ached to see the baby and he ached to hold her vivacious mother in his arms once again. How could he have let her go? He should have resisted his father's warnings to forget the woman. That he didn't step forward and forbid his father to cause harm to Gillianne was unforgivable.

What kind of a man would wish such a thing? If he had it to do over he would have wrapped his arms around her that night in the restaurant when she said goodbye. Her eyes sparkled that evening. He had since come to the conclusion that she was going to tell him she was pregnant, that they had created a baby. But he had quashed any thought she may have had to reveal her pregnancy with his sudden announcement that he was running for the Senate, and, more to the point, that he and Bernadette had reconciled.

"Fool. You were a fool, Maxime," he whispered, chastising his unforgivable actions. He couldn't turn back the clock. But maybe he could make amends. Maybe, just maybe he could persuade her to come back to Paris. Divorce Bernadette? Why not? She only wanted his money. His family's money. He could see to it that she was taken care of for life, maybe not in the lifestyle she thought she was entitled to, but a good one nonetheless.

"Oh, Gillianne, my beautiful, beautiful Gillianne, how can I convince you that we should be together, a family with a baby girl?"

Chapter 7

Seattle

The morning sun breached the building next door to Skip's condo sending a beam through the window hitting him in the eye. His Basset Hound Agatha tugged on his bed covers trying to roust him to take her outside.

"Come on, Aggie, two more minutes."

The blanket fell on the floor followed by a soft bark.

Skip swung his feet to the floor, gave Aggie a pat on the head, and dressed in his jogging pants. Today was his first day of training to run the Seattle marathon in November. Maybe.

Skip Hunter, twenty-nine, kept his six-foot body in top condition—diet, free weights and cardiovascular workouts. His frame was hard as steel. Some said he was too thin. His retort was always, "You're just jealous."

A runner in college he had participated in three marathons and placed in the top ten of each. Of course, this marathon would be different—he was seven years older. But he felt training for a marathon would help clear his head, give him a goal. And training usually provided a breakthrough in any problem that was plaguing him. He hadn't committed to running the Seattle marathon yet which was always held the first Sunday after Thanksgiving. He had a couple of months before the actual preliminary training would begin—

preliminary training to get his muscles and bones toughened for the intense sixteen-week training program his college coach swore by.

With Agatha in tow he headed out of the building and down the driveway to the park. The first mile consisted of jogging, stopping occasionally when Agatha insisted there was something unusual in the grass beside the park's running path. Then there were a few obligatory stops to relieve herself coupled with greeting her buddy, a St. Bernard who put up with her sniffing. Of course there was always a poop session or two, which Skip quickly picked up with a plastic bag and deposited in the nearest trash can.

He finished the first mile, took Agatha home to eat, drink, and sleep on her bed for a doggie dream. Strapping on his heart monitor, swinging a backpack over his shoulders that held two water bottles, he set off again for a two-mile run.

Today he trekked up and down Seattle's streets, some with more than a twenty-degree incline. At this point in his training, he was running at an easy pace. It all depended on his route. Slower today because he was doing the hills.

He had two issues he was dealing with and frankly admitted he didn't know how to proceed with either one. His novel on the Wellington gold heist was at a dead end. So far he had written the background on Eleanor Wellington's arrest—how she and Gerald Sacco smuggled the gold bars to Mexico. The gold had since been found and returned to Wellington minus two million dollars the pair had spent.

Eleanor had been arrested on a yacht in Monaco and was serving time in a Seattle prison, not for the theft, which she had no part in, but for hiding and spending the gold. However, she would soon be released unless the authorities could prove she had killed Gerald Sacco who went missing out in the Mediterranean. The dead end. Unless Skip could find out how Sacco died, the last man alive who participated in the heist, he couldn't finish the book.

And then there was Gilly. Oh, she was pleasant enough when they were together but he wasn't looking for pleasant. In talking to Nicole and Gabby privately, they had innocently told him that Gilly had changed since she returned from Paris from her six months of interning at various fashion houses. But what girl wouldn't change, they argued, if she found herself pregnant and unmarried?

They had hoped that after the baby was born she would lighten up, but instead she became the opposite. She had turned into a control freak. She was involved in every little detail of the business. Not that

Nicole and Gabby minded. Their discussions about the business were always stimulating. They didn't mind that she kept asking questions after they had started implementing a decision. But, they were worried about the future as the company grew. Other employees might not enjoy her meddling.

As a result of talking with the two women Skip toyed with the idea of running in the November marathon. He had to have something that challenged his mind and body until he could break through the wall that Gilly had built around her. Maybe he would never be able to break through but he wasn't ready to give up. However, he was not going to wait forever. There was an end to his patience.

He had also begun to write a second expose—Edward Churchill. What made a young man from a wealthy family in New York City, steal the fashion designs from a wannabe designer—Gilly. Then finding out she's pregnant he proceeds with a double blackmail without either party aware that the other was also being blackmailed. As soon as Churchill's trial was over and he was sentenced, Skip felt he would be able to write that story.

Struggling to the top of the hill, he stopped, bent over, and inhaled deeply as he took his pulse. His heart rate was elevated higher than it should be. Another indication he wasn't in quite the great shape he thought he was. He ambled back to his condo, took a quick shower, and then drove to the newspaper and his crime beat to find out what criminal activity had taken place in the city during the night.

The newsroom was quiet. Reporters kept their heads down in anticipation of the weekend, bracing themselves in the event they were sent out on an assignment. Approaching his cubicle Skip heard two sharp rings from his phone, snatching the receiver on the third ring.

"Hunter."

"Ah, Monsieur Hunter. You know of the Lady Margaret?" the male voice asked.

"The yacht? Monaco?"

"Good, good. I am in possession of some pictures. Pictures I believe you will find interesting."

"Who are you?"

"I'll get to that, Monsieur."

"What kind of pictures?" Skip flopped into his chair, leaned his elbows on his desk, as he bent his head down concentrating on the voice. French. His pen twisted erratically between his fingers.

"Pictures of a woman on the Lady Margaret. A woman with her drunken companion at the rail of the Lady Margaret."

"Go on. What are they doing?"

"Ah, yes. What they are doing is quite damning—for them both."

"Listen, mister, stop wasting my time. You either have something of interest or you don't. Maybe you were hallucinating."

"Monsieur Hunter, I believe you would find the pictures fascinating. So fascinating that you would be willing to buy the pictures—say, a thousand dollars apiece?"

"Where are you?" Skip asked writing the caller ID number on his desk pad.

"France."

"Give me the name of the woman in the picture and then we'll talk."

"She chartered the Lady Margaret under an assumed name, Elaine Winters, but her real name is Eleanor Wellington."

"Listen, mister, why call me now? It's been almost a year since Mrs. Wellington was arrested. She's about to be released. If you have evidence of something that happened when her companion fell overboard and drowned why didn't you give it to the police at the time? I ask again, why now? And why me? I don't have that kind of money."

"Time, Monsieur. There are some things that grow more valuable given time. Don't you agree, Monsieur Hunter? You see I read the Seattle Times. You wrote an article not long ago about what you believed was an unsolved case. Of course, you don't really know if there was a crime. Must be driving you and Mr. Philip Wellington crazy, especially Monsieur Wellington. So crazy that I believe Monsieur Wellington would pay almost anything to put his adulterous, thieving, and perhaps murderous wife in prison for the rest of her life. Wouldn't you agree with me, Monsieur Hunter?"

Skip checked the caller ID display for the third time.

"Monsieur Hunter, are you there?"

"Yeah, yeah." Skip stood, pushed his chair back with his leg, stroked his buzz cut. Was this guy for real, he wondered? Was the evidence for the climax of his exposé somewhere on the other end of this line?

"By the way, forget about tracing the telephone number," the voice whispered. "It's disposable. Now, why don't you talk to Monsieur Wellington? Of course, every day that goes by the price goes up."

"Look, let's say Mr. Wellington is interested. He would have to have proof you really have something of interest and that you aren't trying to extort money from him."

"Yes, I can give you proof. Talk to Monsieur Wellington. I'll call you back tomorrow for his answer, but of course that's another day so the price is now two-thousand dollars—each picture."

Skip hung up the receiver at the drone of the disconnected call.

Chapter 8

It had been two months since the fire and, if all went according to the contractor's schedule, the shop would be finished next week. The investigation into the cause of the fire had cleared the Sinclairs and Gilly and her staff. However, the investigation continued. The police and the various insurance companies involved acknowledged the forensic results proving the fire was the work of an arsonist, but the question remained: who struck the match?

Contractors quickly swarmed the little shop and the upstairs loft. Gilly pressed the general contractor to put all his efforts into completing the work on the shop first allowing her to open the doors for business. Gillianne Wilder Fashions desperately needed some sales. She oversaw every aspect of the work, lying out exactly what she wanted but within the money allowed under the insurance policy. Gabby and Maria—sales and marketing—continually huddled with Gilly offering ideas. She agreed with many, adopted most, but always had the final say.

Gabby continued to change the front windows tantalizing pedestrians to stop, press their noses to the glass, hands cupped around their faces so they could see the interior, wave at a workman, and then amble on.

Gilly maintained control of the project and her directions were absolute. Robyn remained her first priority and the center of her attention, but the business was a close second. Robyn's new bassinet was placed close to the conference table but this morning she was asleep in her crib next to Gilly's bed behind the partitions.

The staff of four plus Gilly met every morning. Before sitting down, they helped themselves to Arthur's freshly brewed pot of coffee.

This morning Gabby spoke first relaying what she had found out about debuting their collection in this fall's New York Fashion Week. "We can't do it."

"And that's because?" Gilly asked.

"*Way* too expensive—over $100,000 is not unusual and most designers spend *way* more than that. And besides the money, in order to participate we have to be selling into several major stores and have significantly more revenue. However, these are all moot points because we missed the deadline. Applications were due by the end of last year."

Gabby looked up from her notes. They all turned to Gilly waiting to see her reaction.

"Okay. Then that becomes our future goal," Gilly said. "Gabby, make a poster with bullets—no more than three or five, listing what we must do to be invited to participate. We'll mount it on the wall." Gilly saw her staff droop. They had been excited at the prospect of going to New York, breaking into the big time. "Just because New York is out of reach … for the moment … doesn't mean we tread water. We move to plan B."

Nicole smiled brightly. "Tell us about plan B. What are we going to do?"

"California. Los Angeles. Spring Fashion Week next March—showing our fall collection. The registration form must be submitted by the end of June."

Gabby smiled. Gilly had asked her to prepare plan B in advance of this morning's staff meeting. Gilly had not only embraced the idea, she was off and running with it.

"We'll have a fresh new collection. Here, look at these. Tell me what you think." Gilly quickly walked to a stack of small posters she had mounted on foam core boards, standing them up on an eight-foot strip of molding she had asked one of the workers to tack to the wall. There were twenty-three posters depicting the new fall collection.

"Come on. What do you think? And, I want your honest assessment. Is it a start?" Gilly asked.

Gilly had shared her ideas with Gabby as she progressed through the designs—sketches, tweaks, adding and deleting until she saw what she was striving for. Then pausing only to tackle each sketch again. Perfecting. Perfecting. Perfecting. Gabby stood back while Nicole and

Maria scrutinized the drawings from left to right, passing each poster, taking in the lines, the colors.

Arthur topped off his coffee. He knew nothing about fashion. He did know about accounting and he prayed the new collection would bring in some much needed revenue.

Nicole threw her arms around Gilly. "They're terrific. When can we start the samples?"

"Today. Maria, what do you think?"

Maria turned and smiled. "You blow me away. All new and fresh."

"Hey, where is everybody?"

Their heads snapped up as the door at the top of the stairs from the shoe shop swung open.

"Sheridan!" Gilly exclaimed running to embrace her former Paris roommate.

Nicole was next to throw her arms around the New Yorker, and then Gabby kissed both of her former client's cheeks.

"Sheridan, please meet Maria Jackson, my long-time friend, and Arthur Lewis, our accountant."

Gilly pulled Sheridan to the table where she was greeted by Maria and Arthur. "We were discussing our new fall collection. Coffee? How did you find us and why didn't you let us know you were coming?"

"Yes, to the coffee and I expect it to be great after all I've heard about Seattle's coffee, especially Starbuck's lattes."

Arthur had poured a mug of coffee and handed it to Sheridan nodding at the cream and sugar.

"How come you're … in Seattle?" Nicole asked with a giggle.

"When did you leave Paris? Where are you working? You are working aren't you?" Gabby asked.

"Yes. I tried to get a job in the fashion business in New York. But, no such luck. I'm modeling and doing some designing at a small company in Los Angeles."

"We were just talking about LA," Gilly said. "Tell us how you ended up there and about this company you're working for."

"Excuse me, ladies," Arthur said. "I have some bookwork to do. Nice to meet you, Sheridan."

"Nice to meet you, too, Arthur."

"Gilly, I'm going to work from home today. If there's anything you need, give me a call."

"Can't take all the female chatter huh?" Gilly asked with a little wave as Arthur smiled sheepishly and left.

"How long are you going to be in town?" Gabby asked.

"Oh, a day or two." Sheridan said adding a small container of cream and then taking a sip of her coffee. She looked over the edge of her mug at her former agent.

"Good. I'm afraid Maria and I have to duck out. We have an appointment with a buyer and then Maria has to pick up a special lookbook she's been working on. Gilly, how about we treat Sheridan to dinner tonight down on the waterfront?"

"Good idea. See you two later."

"Make that three," Nicole said. "I have an appointment with Vinsenso at the factory." She hugged Sheridan again and dashed down the stairs after Maria and Gabby.

It was suddenly quiet. Sheridan looked at Gilly. "Okay, start at the top and fill me in about the shop. But first where is the baby? I still can't believe you didn't nail that creep Maxime for support."

"She's due to wake up," Gilly said ignoring Sheridan's barb. Robyn is none of her business, she thought. "Let me go get her. It's time for her bottle anyway. I'll be right back as soon as I change her. I can't believe you're here, Sheridan. It's so good to see you."

Gilly quickly walked to the other side of the large space and disappeared down a hallway of partitions.

Sheridan stepped over to the wall to get a closer look at the posters of Gilly's collection. Fishing in her handbag for her cell, she clicked the button, one-by-one, taking a picture of each poster as she passed. She smiled as she took the pictures. They were just what she and Zak needed. Her two-person company was going under.

Bitter at not being hired in New York after all the hours she had spent interning in Paris, she had struck up a friendship with Zak Foster in a bar. They had shared a drink, and then smoked some marijuana as they walked the streets commiserating over their jobless plight. Zak suggested they hook up and go to LA where he was sure her designs would catch the eye of lots of buyers. She would design and he would manage the business—the money side. Of course, Sheridan, a beautiful twenty-seven, five-foot-ten woman with long silky black hair, could still do some modeling to bring in extra moola.

One night sitting outside in the ally in back of their LA shop, she told him about her months in Paris and how her supposed friends, her roommates, had formed an alliance without her. So, of course, together they had to be making scads of money. As they talked they enjoyed a snort of coke and she decided her former friends owed her. Zak wholeheartedly agreed and suggested if they were making so much dough, they would be oblivious to a few copies of their designs surfacing in California.

Glancing over her shoulder to see if Gilly was returning with the baby, Sheridan quickly retraced her steps snapping an additional set of pictures. Dropping her phone in her large shoulder bag, she poured herself another mug of coffee and again strolled along the wall of posters.

"Here she is. Her name is Robyn. Isn't she the cutest little person ever?" Gilly asked kissing the mop of red curls as Robyn, now almost three months old, cooed and patted her mother's cheek.

Chapter 9

A strong rap announced a visitor as the loft door swung open. Startled, Gilly and Sheridan jerked around as Skip sauntered into the design studio. He kissed Gilly on the cheek lifting Robyn from her arms. Tickling the baby's tummy, he sent her into squeals of delight resulting in the hiccups.

"Well, that's quite an entrance," Gilly said. "Skip, I'd like you to meet my Paris roommate, Sheridan—

"We've met," Skip cut in. "What brings you to Seattle, Sheridan? I thought you were a New Yorker."

Gilly watched the two, their eyes signaling more than just recognition. Skip had planned on surprising Gilly in Paris, but it turned out he was the one surprised. She was in Monaco and Milan that weekend. The weekend Robyn was conceived. Sheridan and Nicole had covered for her, not letting on to Skip that she was spending the weekend with another man. It was also the weekend when on her return, her roommates told her Maxime was married.

At this moment neither Sheridan nor Skip said anything more about their meeting other than recognizing it had occurred.

"Nice to see you again, Skip. I'm working in LA. Not much available in New York at the moment," Sheridan said extending her hand.

Skip gave it a quick shake and sat down cradling Robyn as she played with his tie.

"I have to be going," Sheridan said rising and pulling on her sweater.

"You don't have to go, Sheridan," Gilly said glancing at Skip.

"I have a couple of appointments. Cute kid. See you later for dinner, Gilly."

Gilly and Skip watched the door close behind Sheridan and then turned to face each other.

"I forgot you two met. What's up? I haven't seen you for a few weeks," Gilly said. "Coffee?"

"Not today. I dropped by to tell you that I'm leaving for Paris in the morning."

"What for?" Gilly tensed. Why Paris, she thought? The mere suggestion of the city caused her pulse to quicken.

"I had a call … a tipster. He says he has some pictures he wants to sell to Wellington. From the sounds of it, it may be the evidence Wellington and DuBois, as well as myself, have been waiting for. They may show Eleanor helping Sacco off the yacht to his death. At least that's what we're hoping for."

"I see. That would be good for you wouldn't it? You might get the ending to your exposé you've been waiting for. I hope for both of your sakes, and Mr. Wellington's, that they show something that DuBois can use as evidence."

"Me, too. And, I also stopped by to let you know that I'm running again."

"Running?"

"Yeah, like training to run in this year's Seattle Marathon."

"You look good." Suddenly flustered, she added, "I mean trim, well, you always look trim. You know what I mean."

"I know what you mean, but it's fun to watch you try to say that you're looking," he said with a grin spreading on his face."

"When's the race?"

"It's always held the first Sunday after Thanksgiving. I'll print a course map for you. Maybe you can cheer me on." Again he grinned, enjoying that he was making her uncomfortable, a person who always maintained her control, at least since she returned from Paris pregnant. "You could hand me a bottle of water at mile sixteen," he teased.

"A marathon is hard isn't it? Twenty-six miles?"

"Twenty-six point two to be precise, Ms. Wilder." He held Robyn's little red curls next to his face. "Maybe if you're good your mommy will bring you to see me run," he whispered into the baby's ear causing her to giggle and another round of the hiccups.

"Here, I'll take her. I have a bottle of water."

"I've got her. Go get the water."

Gilly returned and put the warmed bottle into Skip's outstretched hand.

"What do you do to train? And didn't you say you won a marathon in college?" Gilly asked.

"Ah, your mommy was listening to me when I told her about my big win in Oklahoma." Robyn was fixated on Skip's face as she sucked on her bottle cradled in his arms.

"First, I dusted off my training journals from that year, and, yes, I finished first. That was the only one, however. Placed fourth and fifth in two other marathons. This time, for me, it's not so much winning the race but proving that I can run the distance. So ... just to let you know that I'll be waiting for you until the end of the race, until the hoopla is over."

"Waiting for me?"

Skip looked up from Robyn's dark button eyes and at Gilly, her green eyes questioning what he was saying.

"Yes, waiting for you, Gilly. If you still have yourself walled off, a wall so thick I haven't been able to break through, then it will be time for me to move on."

As Skip left he flipped the lock on the door, looked back at Gilly and Robyn, and shut the door. Always the protector.

"Hey, Zak, it's me."

"About time you called, Sheridan. Did you see anything of interest?"

"Oh, yeah. Zak, baby, we're back in business. Just wait 'til I show you. We'll have a snorting good time when I get back tomorrow night."

Chapter 10

It was a day of surprises. First, Sheridan arrives unannounced—a big surprise, but even more shocking was that the hardcore New Yorker had taken a job on the west coast leaving Paris for Los Angeles. Then, while the former roommates shared a cup of coffee in the loft, Skip knocked, walked in after a two-week absence, and laid down an ultimatum—get off your high-horse by Thanksgiving or he was not going to be around to pick up the pieces any longer.

Now alone in the loft, the sun passing its arc sending shadows creeping over the floorboards, Gilly shed her black jacket tossing it on her bed and adjusted her white blouse under the waistband of her black trousers. She pulled the coverlet up to Robyn's chin, kissed the sleeping infant, and backed away from her crib returning to the studio side of the partitions.

Hearing a knock, she wondered who would be visiting this time. She walked to the door, flipped the lock, and pulled it open.

Stunned, she grasped the edge of the door for support.

"Gillianne, you are more beautiful than I remembered. I could not bear to wait any longer. Forgive me, s'il vous plaît, for not calling first. I … I was afraid you might turn me away."

Maxime stood in the doorway, a bouquet of red roses in his hand, his dark eyes pleading, warm, and full of love and apprehension that she might very well turn him away. His black suit fit his large six-foot-one frame perfectly, his white silk shirt open at the neck.

"Gillianne, I was a fool. Can I come in? Just a little while? See our baby?"

Gilly leaned her head on the steel, fire proof door, holding the edge with both hands.

Our baby!

She willed herself to breathe, inhaling deep breaths, gathering strength. Backing away from the door she weakly waved her hand for him to enter.

Maxime walked through the door stopping on the other side of the threshold, afraid to reach out. She looked as if any sudden move on his part she might shatter.

Gilly slowly walked away from the open door and Maxime. She looked across the loft to the window. A bird sat on the sill looking back at her. Continuing to breathe deeply she tamped down the tension that held her. How dare he arrive at her doorstep without so much as a letter, a note, a call.

Maxime laid the bouquet of roses on the conference table, giving her time ... time to do what? Throw him out?

Gilly turned to face him. He was standing ten feet from her ... a world away. "Congratulations, *Senator*." Her green eyes sparking as she said the words. "I imagine your *wife* is pleased with the outcome of the election."

There, she thought, the last words he said to me that night in Paris but this time I'm skewering him.

"Can we talk, Gillianne? There is so much I have to say. I—"

"Maxime." She took another breath. The mere saying of his name catching in her throat. "Maxime," she tried again. "There is nothing you can say that I want to hear. You've made the trip for nothing."

"Maybe in time you will forgive me, let me into your life. I wish to hear how you're doing, how our child is doing. Gillianne, I always wanted a baby, even like this I consider her to be a miracle. The days we spent in Milan ... Monaco ... my dear beautiful Gillianne, she was conceived at that time. We loved each other. I can't presume you could ever love me again that way, but I dream of it, of you, of ... let me see her. I beg you."

Excited chatter and laughter preceded Nicole and Gabby as they burst through the open doorway. Nicole stopped, held her arm out stopping Gabby from passing her, her eyes wide in alarm looking from Maxime to Gilly to Maxime and back to Gilly. She grasped Gabby's hand, rooting her to her side. "Are you all right, Gilly?" she whispered her eyes continuing to dart between the pair standing in front of her.

"Yes. Maxime dropped by. How about that? All the way from Paris … he dropped by. Maxime, this is Nicole, my roommate in Paris, and Gabby my agent. They know all about you. Actually, it was Nicole who let the cat out of the bag that you were married. In fact, she dropped that little bombshell shortly after we parted at the airport on our return from our *romantic* weekend in Milan. Fancy that."

Maxime turned back to Gilly. "The baby."

"Nicole, Gabby, please come in but leave the door open. As I said, Maxime is about to leave. But before he leaves, he wants to see *my* baby. What do you think?"

Nicole raised her shoulders.

"Maxime, if you see the baby, you'll leave?" Gilly asked.

"Yes, Gillianne, I will leave." He stood his ground. For all his sweet words he still presented a powerful, determined, figure. But he made no threatening move, nor were his words said in a demanding tone. But, he was firm in his request.

"Gabby and Nicole, please wait here while I get Robyn." Gilly took a tentative step. Her legs didn't buckle. Inhaling another deep breath, she walked through the partitioned hallway with firm strides, and stood beside the crib. Gripping the rail she shut her eyes. Do I have to do this, she wondered?

With another deep breath, Gilly quickly picked up the sleeping baby, wrapped the blanket around her, held her tight against her breasts, kissed her mop of red curls and retraced her footsteps.

Standing in front of Maxime, she folded the soft pink blanket back so he could see Robyn's little face. She opened her eyes, looked at the man in front of her, her big dark eyes looking into a matching pair crinkling at the edges as a smile slowly filled his face.

"Ma petite princesse. Belle, belle. Précieuse. Les boucles rouges comme ta maman." Maxime whispered. He opened his hands to Gilly. "May I hold her?"

Gilly pulled back.

"S'il vous plaît?"

Gilly looked at Gabby. She shrugged in response. It was Gilly's call.

Gilly put the baby in Maxime's large hands. He gazed down at his daughter, touched a red curl. Robyn batted his chin and grasped his finger. "My little one. Beautiful, beautiful. Red curls like your mother's." He raised the tiny fingers to his lips.

Seeing Maxime's gesture conjured up the image of the many times he had kissed her hand. She swiftly lifted her daughter from his arms and backed away.

"Goodbye, Maxime."

Ironic, she thought. She just said the words she had uttered as she left him standing in the Paris restaurant after he had told her he was running for the Senate and that he and his wife had reconciled.

"Au revoir. I love you … and our beautiful baby. Merci. I will keep in touch." Maxime nodded to Gabby and Nicole, turned, for one last glimpse at Gillianne holding their baby, paused and then he was gone.

Chapter 11

Paris

Three men, dressed in suits and ties, strode across the elegant Place Vendôme, between the Garnier Opera House and the Louvre, then under the white canopy and through the glass doors of the Ritz Carlton. The youngest man of the three approached the maître de l'hôtel at the Vendôme Bar. "My name is Skip Hunter. My companions and I have a lunch appointment with a man we have never met. Has—"

"Ah, yes, Monsieur Hunter. Follow me, s'il vous plaît."

Hunter, DuBois, and Wellington followed the man through the sumptuously appointed bar. Rich terra-cotta walls, carpet, upholstery under a polished wood cantilevered ceiling provided a warm atmosphere and backdrop for tables covered with white linen. A single pink flower circled with green leaves in a small crystal vase, and crystal salt and pepper shakers were centered on each table. The bar opened at 10:30 a.m. It was now 10:35.

A man sitting in an oval booth watched the gentlemen approach. His lips turned up slightly as he recognized two of the three men. The man remained seated casually taking another sip of his double martini.

The maître de l'hôtel left the men as they stood facing the man—sitting, grinning up at them.

"You're expecting us?" Skip asked.

The man nodded, maintaining his grin.

"I recognize you. You're the steward I saw on the Lady Margaret, but I don't know your name. What is it?" Skip asked.

"Monsieur Charles de Gaulle."

"Very funny," DuBois said in a low voice. "What's your real name, pal or we're leaving. We didn't spend almost two days traveling here to play games."

"Ah, Detective? I am right, yes?"

"Yes. Your turn."

"Monsieur Sean Lacroix, at your service. Have a seat, s'il vous plaît."

The men settled in the booth as a waiter stepped to the table and accepted their drink orders. The men said nothing, waiting for their drinks—a fresh martini for Lacroix, scotch for Wellington, and water for DuBois and Hunter—and the departure of the waiter before they spoke.

Lacroix, looking over the edge of his glass, asked, "You must be Monsieur Wellington?"

"Yes, and let's get on with this. We all know why we're here. Give us the pictures," Wellington demanded.

"Not yet. I have seven prints in my jacket pocket. I will show you two of them. But, first you will give me $5000."

"We settled on $2000 each. Two pictures—$4000," Skip whispered angrily.

"Oh, that was days ago, Monsieur. The price is now $2500 each. A bargain I assure you."

Wellington opened a leather wallet and handed Lacroix three traveler's checks—$2000 each. "Here's six thousand—a thousand on account for the third picture," Wellington said.

Lacroix reached into his inside jacket pocket retrieving two pictures and laid them in front of Wellington.

The pictures were dark. Two figures were illuminated by three candles on a nearby table. The candlelight was enough to identify Eleanor Wellington holding up Gerald Sacco as he leaned against her. She had a hand on his foot. His foot was on the lower rail circling the yacht's aft deck. The other picture was more than likely taken seconds later showing Sacco hanging out over the water.

Without saying a word, Wellington opened his wallet again, counted out three more traveler's checks and laid them on the table in front of Lacroix—six thousand in his pocket and another six on the table. Lacroix reached for the traveler's checks but Wellington quickly set the crystal vase with the pink flower on top of the checks keeping his fingers around the vase.

"Show us all the pictures. If they are as you say, you will receive $18,000—seven pictures at $2500 a piece is $17,500 a large sum. If, and that's a big if, they divulge as much as the first two, you will have a nice tip of $500. Now let's see them." Wellington, fingers still holding the vase, looked into Lacroix's eyes daring him to hand over the pictures.

Lacroix reached again into his jacket pocket and handed the packet of five additional photos to Wellington.

Wellington withdrew his hand from the vase. Lacroix quickly picked up the checks as Wellington scanned each picture handing them in turn to DuBois, and then on to Skip. Without a word, Wellington again reached into his wallet and handed the additional checks to Lacroix.

DuBois narrowed his eyes. "Mr. Lacroix, how did you get these pictures?"

"I took them. At the time I knew the couple as Elaine Winters and Gordon Silvers. To be honest, I was taken with Elaine. Excuse me, Monsieur Wellington, but your wife was a looker, a beautiful woman. And, she knew it. Flaunted her body. It's no wonder that poor Gordon Silvers followed her to the rail, drunk as he was. Anyway, I had taken several pictures of her during the day, on the lounger, almost naked."

Wellington showed no emotion. He drained his scotch and signaled the waiter to bring him another.

"Anybody on that yacht could have taken these pictures. Why should we believe you?" Skip asked.

"Well, you see, I have the camera ... all the pictures." Lacroix glanced at Wellington. Grinned at Wellington. "Want to see 'em?" Lacroix, said with a lecherous look.

DuBois answered for Wellington. "I want to see them. You have the camera with you I presume?"

"As a matter of fact, I do. I thought maybe you would like to see the rest," Lacroix said grinning as he jammed his hand into his right jacket front pocket. "Of course, we'll have to come to an agreement on how much they're worth," he said opening his hand to tantalize the detective, closing it quickly around the small camera.

"Let me see what you have and we'll discuss it," DuBois said.

Lacroix put the small camera into Dubois's outstretched palm. DuBois handed it to Skip. He turned it on and advanced a few frames. He nodded to DuBois and handed the camera to Wellington.

"Mr. Lacroix, I can't pay you for the pictures on the camera," DuBois said. "A defense lawyer would certainly argue against your credibility, and say that I *bought* your testimony. However, what Mr. Wellington does is his business. And, if Mr. Wellington gave us the pictures and the camera then a prosecutor would surely see that they were entered into evidence ... provided you testify as to how you obtained the pictures."

Lacroix smiled. "Let's see, that means I have to travel to the States ... on your dime ... or at least Monsieur Wellington's dime. Is that right?"

"Yes," DuBois said. "That's right. But we will also take the camera with us. Now!"

"Oh, I don't know," Lacroix said looking up at the ceiling, then back at DuBois. "I suppose you can take it for another six grand. Now!" He grinned at Wellington who finished advancing the pictures.

"Excuse me a minute, Mr. Lacroix. Skip, stay with our friend here while I have a chat with Mr. Wellington." DuBois nodded toward the bar.

Perching on a barstool, DuBois looked straight ahead at the mirror. "Philip, we would have a stronger case if we had a video of this guy giving his story, his deposition."

"I agree, Mirage. Can the local police handle that for us?"

"Yes, but, if we involve the locals they might want in on the case, muddy it up. After all Eleanor was arrested in Monaco. It would be cleaner, quicker, if we took Lacroix's deposition in Seattle. However, he'll probably ask for an additional incentive, if you catch my drift."

"Yes, I catch your drift."

"With the pictures and his deposition, I think the prosecutor could go for a murder indictment."

"I see. By all means, let's do it!" Wellington said.

Returning to the table, DuBois addressed Lacroix. "It may be a few months before Mrs. Wellington's trial. However, I'm sure a videotape of your deposition would suffice. What are you doing for the next few days, Mr. Lacroix?"

"Why nothing that matters, Detective. What do you have in mind?"

"I'd like you to come back to Seattle with us ... a quick trip."

Wellington reached again for his wallet, and laid three more checks in front of Lacroix.

"Yes, I can do that," he said pocketing the checks. "Of course, I would need money for expenses. You know—strange city. Clothes. I would need a new suit … for the video. When are you leaving?"

"Right now," DuBois said. "I bought an open ticket for you. I thought if you had what you said you had, that you might be willing to return with us." This time it was DuBois who smiled at Lacroix.

Wellington nodded to a waiter hovering a short distance away. "Gentlemen," Wellington said, "I don't know about you but I feel like having a hearty lunch before we leave. My treat. I've heard the food is pretty good here … at the Ritz."

Chapter 12

Paris

Looking out of his office window at the sparkling waters of the Seine flowing by, Maxime gazed at a tourist boat filled with people falling in love with the city and each other. He was due at his Senate office in thirty minutes but his thoughts were not on his new position, they were in Seattle. A year had gone by since he and Gillianne had made a baby. Seeing her holding their daughter in her arms stirred a yearning in his heart he had not been prepared for.

The infant was a product of their love, receiving the beauty of her mother but the intensity, and warmth of her father. It was all Maxime could do that afternoon to keep from wrapping both mother and child in his arms, never to let them go again. How was he going to undo the unforgivable? The love for Gillianne and Robyn burned into the very core of his being.

There was one thing he had to do immediately.

Marching down the hall, he barged into his father's office. The Count was on the phone but seeing the expression on his son's face, he ended the call. He waited for Maxime to speak, to tell him what caused the unprecedented intrusion.

Maxime paced to the window, then whirled around to face his father.

"Have you ended the business with that detective in Seattle?" His lawyer's voice was controlled, but firm, as if asking a crucial question of a witness demanding an answer.

"No!"

"Call him, now. Tell him his final payment is in the mail."

"Why? What happened? You return from a trip to Germany and suddenly want to cut off the business in Seattle?"

"I didn't go to Germany. I went to Seattle."

"Now you're going to tell me that you want to bring your mistress and her child to Paris?" His father looked at his bookcase full of law books and shook his head. "Maxime, you—

"Call him! Now! I want to hear you tell him. I know you have his cell. Now!"

The Count reached for his phone as he scanned a little black book of numbers lying on his desk. He stabbed his fingers on the phone's buttons. Maxime walked out the door and picked up the startled secretary's phone pushing the lighted button to connect to the same line as his father. Stretching the cord, Maxime stood in the doorway to his father's office—watched him as he listened to the conversation. It ended quickly.

The Count returned the receiver to the cradle as did Maxime. He returned to face his father closing the door behind him.

The Count leaned back in his chair, hands clasped over his stomach, and smiled. "So, my son, you are now not only a Senator but a man. It took you awhile but I wouldn't have missed seeing you in action for anything. You didn't answer my question. Are you planning to move your little family to Paris?"

Maxime turned away from his father, again facing the window. "No. She wouldn't come if I asked her. She hates me. Wants nothing to do with me."

"Then that's it?"

"No, that's not it. I'm not sure how, but I want to be part of her life. I want the baby to know her father, know that he's not a monster. I dream of Gillianne forgiving me, loving me again, I'll try everything I know to win her respect, her love, her forgiveness. But I don't think she will ever give me her heart again, and I can't say as I blame her."

"And Bernadette?"

"I'm going to divorce her."

The Count laughed. "My, my. You love one woman but she doesn't love you. You want to divorce another woman who will never grant you such a thing. I'd say you have your work cut out for you. Let's go have lunch at the Ritz. This is a special occasion and we must start it off right. I want to watch my son, the Senator, to see how he is going to solve these problems of his heart."

"No thanks. I'm due in Parliament—there's a special session today. I've prepared an argument and I must give it."

Maxime strode to the door, his hand on the knob. "I start today, this moment, to throw myself into my duties and to begin a new campaign. A different campaign. One that seems impossible, but I will try with ever fiber of my being. A campaign to win Gillianne's trust and hopefully her love."

Chapter 13

Hansville

Gramps sat at the kitchen table with a cup of tea reading the morning Seattle Times. The headline: *Eleanor Wellington indicted for Murder*.

What was that? Gramps cocked his head, brow furrowed. Did he hear a car door slam?

A dog barked, more of a howl. A big smile crossed Gramp's face. Agatha was howling at the patio door for her friend. Skip trotted down the garden steps as Gramps opened the patio door and was almost bowled over by the hound.

"Hi, Gramps," Skip said laughing at the pair. "I hoped you'd be home."

"Just a minute, Skip. My friend wants a belly rub. Go on in, the water's hot. You know where the teabags are."

Agatha, four paws in the air was playing dead enjoying her belly rub. Having enough she squirmed to her feet and dashed after her master into the kitchen. She was greeted by a hissing cat, both backing away from each other. Aggie took up her spot in the doorway as Coco tippy-toed out of the kitchen.

"Just reading your story," Gramps called out padding down the hall to join Skip. "Now you tell me the good stuff. What murder?"

Skip poured the water from the red enamel kettle over the teabag into his cup, nodded to Gramps as he raised the kettle to see if he wanted to refresh his cup.

"Yes, please," Gramps answered, a smile above his white whiskers, pants held up with red suspenders over a long-sleeve green plaid shirt.

"Received a tip … from Paris," Skip said settling into a chair at the table while glancing out at the sparkling water of Puget Sound through the picture window. Out of the corner of his eye he imagined Gilly sitting beside him. He could almost smell her perfume.

"Paris?"

Gramp's question pulled Skip from his reverie. "I didn't know it was Paris at first. Anyway, I returned a few days ago with Detective DuBois. You remember him?"

"Sure I do."

"Turned out my tipster saw Mrs. Wellington help Gerald Sacco, Mr. Wellington's former property manager, over the rail of a yacht way out at sea. Not only did this guy see her but he took pictures of her in the act."

"That must have been almost a year ago," Gramps said taking a sip of his tea.

"The steward, Sean Lacroix, waited. Maybe the police had enough already to convict her, was his thinking, in which case he wouldn't get much for the pictures. But when he read the story I wrote for the paper that she was to be set free for lack of evidence in a few months, he pounced. Decided to come forward. For a price, you understand. He found out Mr. Wellington was wealthy, learned about the gold heist and ultimately sold the pictures to Wellington for big bucks. Eleanor's lawyer is trying to plead that it was an accident, that Sacco fell overboard. Still, she waited over an hour before notifying the captain that he was missing. Her lawyer is trying to save her from the death penalty."

"Nice work, son. Now you can finish that novel of yours—maybe get a Pulitzer."

"Yeah, yeah, a Pulitzer." Skip looked askance but immediately smiled. "But you're right about my finishing the book. When I leave here it will be back to the keyboard—more chapters, editing, then at some point trying to get a publisher. I tackled my laptop last night, but this morning the beginning of June called me outside to go for a run."

"Gilly described you as a runner when we first met you ... oh my, over two years ago?"

"I ran a couple of marathons in college and recently decided to train for the Seattle Marathon."

"When's that? Thanksgiving some time?" Gramps asked.

"First Sunday after. As I said, I was hoping you would be home so Agatha could have some playtime with you while I clock a few miles."

Gramps looked over at his friend. Agatha was in her favorite spot—back half of her body in the living room and the front half in the kitchen pretending to be asleep waiting for Coco to come back. "She's already zonked out so I doubt that will be too hard although Gilly brought Coco here so maybe the two will remember they were friends once. I might even take Agatha for a walk. How long you expect to be gone?"

"I checked the mileage driving here from the ferry. I'm doing preliminary training now trying to get the bones and muscles toughened up. I planned on three or four miles. On Hansville road when I passed the Eglon town sign, it was three miles to your house. I won't go as far as the sign today, make a round trip but at a slow jogging pace. So you think you can put up with Agatha for an hour?"

"You bet I can. I'll have a hearty lunch ready for you when you get back. What are you supposed to eat? Seems I read somewhere about pasta being important."

"That's right," Skip chuckled. "When I'm running water is important. I have a couple of bottles in the car. Thanks. I'll see you in about an hour."

Skip hustled out to his Jeep, strapped on his heart monitor and the pedometer he had calibrated to his stride giving him a fairly accurate idea of the distance he was covering. Walking up to the end of the driveway he stopped to stretch for five minutes and then started south down Hansville Road at an easy jogging pace. There were no sidewalks or curbs. The road was fairly level allowing him to stay a little left of center jogging into traffic. Of course, there never were many cars on the road. It was rural country—towering pines separated by fields and pastures with a glimpse now and then of the Puget Sound through the trees.

It felt good to be running again. He had dug out his journals and training manual from the bottom of a box in the back of his closet. The manual laid out a sixteen-week training program. The introduction stressed the need for preliminary training for at least four weeks, more if you hadn't been running for several years. That was him. He figured June and July for the preliminary training and then get with the sixteen-week program the first of August.

Racing to a newspaper story in a car certainly didn't count. Walking up and down the steep hills of Seattle's downtown district, however, should count for something, he thought.

He breathed in the crisp cool country air. The steady sound of his new running shoes slapping the asphalt was music to his ears. His body relaxed with his easy gait, arms bent swinging across his chest in rhythm with his legs. Gilly entered his thoughts. He smiled at the vision of her handing Robyn to him so she could read the latest chapter of his manuscript. That was before the fire. Those brief visits with her ended three months ago—he had no ending to the exposé and she retreated behind a wall again after the fire.

Today he let his thoughts wander to her, but when he started training with longer runs he would have to focus on his goal—to finish the marathon. He didn't care how long it took—his time on the course wasn't his goal. However long it took him to finish was the time it took. He didn't care about anything else—just finishing would give him a big sense of accomplishment, big enough to provide him with the courage to walk away from Gilly if she didn't tear down the barriers and let him in.

A motorcycle whizzed by him, the man and woman waving as they passed. He waved in return. God, it felt good to be out in the morning air. He knew he could do this … but it will be hard, he thought. Not a walk in the park with Agatha. But he could, would, absolutely would keep to his sixteen-week training schedule of running four times a week once he started the program. Three off days were interspersed on the weekly chart to let his body recover. The weekend would be a long run—maybe come to visit Gramps on Saturday or Sunday. The schedule called for a day off before and after the long run at the end of the week. Every weekday of training built up to the long run. There were a few hills on Hansville road—nothing like Seattle though. He'd have to check the route of the Seattle Marathon. He had only run out-of-state marathons until now. Hills could be a killer. What was it they said about Boston? Oh yeah, heartbreak hill. That bugger left a lot of runners by the wayside.

Picking up his pace after the first mile, he pulled one of his water bottles from his backpack and took several swallows without losing his stride.

"Hi, Gramps, I'm back," Skip called out entering the patio as Agatha sashayed over the door sill bumping her tummy. He knelt down and gave his pooch a good scratch behind the ears. Agatha leaned into the massage, nose in the air, eyes closed.

"I'm in the kitchen," Gramps replied.

Skip gave Agatha one last pat on the head and then strode down the hall to the kitchen. Coco scampered across the hall diving under the couch in the living room.

"Wow! Now that's what I call a sandwich," Skip said hands on his hips.

"You'll have to tell me what's best now that you're training for the big run. How'd it go? Not too many cars I hope."

"It was great. Honestly, Gramps, it felt so good. The air was cool and only a few cars. Really helps to clear the mind."

"Your mind need clearing? Tea?"

"Yes, to both. It's that granddaughter of yours."

"Ah. She works too much. Course, I could say the same for you. Now there's a woman who needs her mind swept. Gets me all worked up when I think about it. Doesn't trust anyone. Wants to control everything. That Frenchman really did a number on her."

"Well ... I ..."

"Go ahead, you can talk to me. You what?"

"Gramps, I told her about my training to run the marathon."

"She didn't try to talk you out of it did she?"

"No. Not at all. She seemed supportive. Didn't say much though. But I did. I was in one of those moods where words just fly out of your mouth, pent up words."

"So?"

"So, I told her that after the marathon if she wanted to stay behind the walls she'd built around herself I was going to move on. Not too sure what that means other than I'll try to get her out of my mind. Maybe I'll move away. I don't know."

"She's a fool if she lets you *move on*. She may not see it, but I see a lot of similarities in you two, and what's not alike can add spice to the other's life. Hope it works out. But in the meantime, I had an idea while you were out running."

"What's that? This sandwich is to die for—hard-boiled egg, ham and cheese, lettuce, wheat bread—a runner's dream."

"Well, I hoped you see it that way. You said your training includes a long run on weekends. So why don't you and Aggie come over here on Saturday and Sunday. You can run and work on your novel, and I'll feed the two of you."

"Hey, remember what they say, be careful what you ask for you just might get it. Something like that." Skip peered into Gramp's gray-blue eyes, his rosy cheeks, a wrinkle here and there. He had grown to love this old man as a second father, well, maybe more like a grandfather.

Gramps didn't say anything, took a bite of his sandwich—a much smaller version of Skip's—and waited as Skip mulled over his offer.

"Are you sure we won't be too much trouble? Agatha can be pretty pushy, you know—belly rubs, rawhide bones now and then, and following you around. Always following you."

"Son, I can't think of anything better."

"I could bring over a copy of my training manual. You can be my diet coach. Give me a list of groceries and I'll bring them over with me. You're not going to get stuck with the two of us plus buying the food. And, you *can't* charm Anne into furnishing any of the meals. That would have to be part of the deal."

"Deal? Sounds like heaven. Promoted to a coach, dietitian, and dog pal. What could be better? Of course, if Anne wants to leave something now and then I can't stop her, you understand. You bring your laptop with you?"

"Sure did."

"Then stop wasting time. I cleaned off my desk in the den. It's a little dark in there. If you'd rather have a table in the living room so you can look out at the boat traffic—

"The den will be perfect. Looking out at the water would cause my mind to wander and we both know that would not be good."

Chapter 14

Seattle

Paint brushes, paint cans, rags and scaffolding were carted out to one of several vans parked in the back alley of the little shop. Heavy tarps and drop clothes were rolled up revealing a gleaming honey-oak stained floor. Electricians standing on ladders screwed bulbs into track-lighting strips washing the walls with indirect lighting. Tube lights were snapped into place on the bottom of shelves providing a soft glow inside the space.

Various soft-toned paint colors inside each shelf gave the illusion of items grouped into sections. The edges were painted light pearl gray matching any expanse of wall not supporting a shelf. An accessory wall, pearl gray, supported floating glass shelving spotted with lights from above.

With the exodus of painters, carpenters, electricians and their equipment from the alley, they were quickly replaced with other vans disgorging chrome racks—round, oblong, tiered, rods set in place between and under shelves for smaller items such as scarves, handbags, and shoes. The smell of fresh paint lingered in the air along with the overall scent of newness from the fixtures.

Robyn sat in a stroller batting a mobile of yellow ducklings as Gilly and her other three mothers, Nicole, Gabby, and Maria, battled to bring order out of chaos.

Nicole took charge of the delivery of two small, glossy-white lacquered bistro tables with matching wrought-iron chairs—three with seats and a circle on the back upholstered in black and white pinstripe fabric and three more in a black and white toile depicting French scenes. The drapery installers arrived and quickly hung pearl-gray tieback curtains in the two front display windows topped with a pink chiffon over black valance.

Gilly had asked Maria to repaint the large shop sign over the windows and front glass door. The new sign, Gillianne Wilder Fashions, painted with gold lettering on black.

Maria stood outside the shop overseeing the painting of the shop's name when a cab drew up to the curb. A handsome woman, blond hair in a French twist, wearing a black silk suit, stepped out of the cab and looked up at the sign. Maria watched the attractive woman overhearing her giving instructions with a decided French accent to the driver. She walked past Maria and through the open door of the shop. Nobody said anything to her as they scurried around installing, moving, positioning and then rearranging items as Gilly directed.

Gilly called out to Gabby to watch Robyn. "I have to run out back for a minute. There's a disagreement over the check Arthur wrote out for the furniture delivery."

"Will do," Gabby called back. She looked over at the stroller and then back to the chrome bar she held for the installer trying to screw in the bracket under a line of shelves.

The woman with the French twist sauntered through the shop, saw the baby, stooped over with her back to the activity behind her and clucked at the infant to get her attention while at the same time taking several pictures with her cell phone.

"Excuse me, Madame. Is there something I can do for you?" Nicole asked squeezing between the woman and the stroller.

"Merci, no, no." The woman smiled, turned away from Nicole and strolled out of the shop and ducked back into the cab. "Hey, who are you?" Nicole asked dodging around the workers trying to catch the woman, but she was already in the cab and it was pulling away from the curb.

"What's the matter, Nicole?" Maria asked. "Touch up the W with a little more of the gold. You missed a spot," she called to the sign painter, her hands cupped around her mouth.

"Nothing, I guess," Nicole replied as she glanced up at the shop's name. "I sure like the gold on black. Gilly was smart to change the colors—more sophisticated." She looked back at the traffic slowing in front of the shop before moving on—gawkers. The cab with the woman was out of sight.

Chapter 15

Los Angeles

With the shop open for business the contractors switched their focus to the second floor—the apartment and design studio. Even with budget constraints necessitated by the smaller than expected insurance payout, there was room and money to construct the two areas. Frills would have to come later—additional lighting, throw rugs on newly refinished oak floors, and replacement one-by-one of the remaining rental furniture.

Gilly decided it was a good time to get away and check out the Los Angeles fashion Week venue—what prices, services, and options were available for various levels of participation. And, most important, make contact with Shirley Stanhope, the event organizer. Gabby had sent in the application form for the following year's March fashion week featuring GWF's fall line. Anne volunteered to take care of her granddaughter for the two days Gilly and Gabby were in LA.

Several events had been scheduled around the fashion district during the week but the CMC, California Market Center, 13th Floor, was where the action occurred as far as the fashion designers were concerned.

The cab pulled up in front of the CMC building—a large streamlined edifice, with tall windows side by side between white cement columns marching up to the top floor.

Shirley Stanhope met the two women in the lobby and whisked them onto the elevator to the 13th floor. Nothing was scheduled at the Center this day, so Gilly and Gabby were able to get a good perspective of the vastness of the space. Shirley gave them a short walk-through and then they sat at a conversation area delineated by a white upholstered curved couch and white cubes serving as tables. White iron chairs faced the couch. Similar conversation areas were scattered throughout the space for visitors, buyers, and designers to discuss the various collections or just to get off their spiked high-heels for a rest.

Shirley opened a sales packet she had put together listing the various options Gillianne Wilder Fashions might want to consider for their debut showing.

"There is a show during fashion week called FOCUS. It is set up to showcase emerging brands and designers. Rates for inclusion in this show start at $900," Shirley said handing Gilly and Gabby a sheet listing the specifics of FOCUS. "We like to think of it as a discovery lab for the press and retailers. The show runs for three days. Depending on what options you choose you can display your collection on mannequins or in a space with a short walkway for the models, or a combination of both." Shirley handed the event folder to Gilly.

"I see you have an exhibit called SELECT?" Gilly said.

"Yes. It's a new tradeshow and the rates start at $3,700. Given what Ms. Dupont, Gabby, said over the phone that this was your first show and money was definitely a factor, I thought FOCUS would give you the most bang for the buck, so to speak," she said with light chuckle. "But, of course, you can do whatever you feel best suits your needs."

"Your guidance is appreciated, Shirley, especially since this is our first show," Gilly said. "My plan is to bring three of my staff to the show in October, your fall event, so we can get a feel for how it works, see what the other designers do to showcase their particular lines, and then go back to the drawing board, so to speak," Gilly said laughing.

"Observing the show in action is the best way to see all aspects, opportunities, if you will. Not only how other designers present their collections but also see the services and how they work—dressing rooms, lounge and reception areas, stages, furniture, audio/visual options."

"What about models, hair and makeup stylists?" Gabby asked.

"I can give you some names but the best way is to roam around backstage at the shows and pickup the business cards of the stylists you like. Also ask the designers what modeling agencies they use. And by all means ask the models themselves what agency represents them. Do they like the agency? You'll find some models freelance for considerably less than what you'll pay an agency. Of course, then you are at their mercy if they don't show up. Many designers participating for the first time in a show will use mannequins to cut the cost … and the headaches."

Gilly thanked Shirley for her help and advice and said goodbye. They exited the mammoth building into the bright, hot sunshine of southern California. Neither said a word as they walked down the street.

Gabby spoke first. "I don't know about you, but I'm in desperate need of a shot of caffeine."

Gilly looked sideways at her friend and nodded. "You can say that again. Looks like a coffee shop across the street. It's not quite Paris but it'll do in a pinch," she laughed. "We'd better watch out for the traffic. The cars really speed around here."

The exhaust from the various size vehicles—cars, vans, trucks, busses—created a haze mixing with the sunshine and emitting a strong odor. At the corner they waited for the stoplight to change so they could cross the six lanes.

"Downtown Seattle could use these wide lanes," Gabby said as they hustled to the other side of the street feeling as though they were taking their lives in their hands.

It was 2:05 and the lunch crowd had evacuated the little café. With a cup of coffee and splitting a turkey sandwich, the girls stared at each other.

"I think we are about to step from a local boutique to … to what? Not really the big time. We can't afford a venue with a runway yet," Gilly said.

"The runway definitely ranks as the big time," Gabby replied. "But, you never can tell who'll drop by, see our line, say at the FOCUS show. And, our fall collection is tailored made for a pitch to the career woman."

Gilly checked her watch. "We have time to drop by Sheridan's company. Do you have her address handy? If not I'll—

"Sit tight. I've got it right here." Gabby pulled out a notepad, flicked through several pages and handed the pad to Gilly.

"She said it wasn't far from the fashion district, which we are sitting in the middle of," Gilly said. "Let's take a cab so we can save time. I'm glad we're spending the night here. I want to do some major poking around other designer's specialty shops. Maybe some have participated in the LA show. Give us some tips."

"Our flight leaves at two tomorrow?" Gabby asked.

"That's right." Gilly paid the lunch tab with the company credit card and then the two, refreshed and a new spring in their step, ventured once again into the smoggy sunshine due to the high humidity settling over the city. "I could take this weather in the winter," Gabby said flagging down a cab.

The cab driver nodded when Gilly gave him the address and sped off merging into traffic. Fifteen minutes later he stopped, ran around to open the door, received payment, and left the girls standing in front of a two-story orange stucco building, attached to a string of identical orange stucco buildings, all looking in need of some repair. The sidewalk had seen better days but the cracks didn't slow down a couple of kids on skateboards, racing down the cement, jumping the board into the street as they passed Gilly and Gabby, and then jumping back onto the sidewalk. Heat rose from the pavement and they heard a police siren in the distance.

Gabby shrugged her shoulders and the pair walked up to the entrance, a heavy metal door between two smudged windows, and stepped inside.

They faced a counter, a ringing telephone, a dingy empty space, and no one in attendance. A thirty-something man rushed out of a hallway and grabbed the telephone almost dropping the receiver at the sight of two women standing inside the front door.

"Yeah. I'll call you back," he said and banged the receiver down.

"Now, what can I do for you two?" His tone wasn't hostile, but he also didn't look happy to see them. His jeans were baggy to the floor, a pair of scuffed sneakers poking from under a cuff. His name, Zak, was stitched in black on a red tank shirt. He took a swipe at his shoulder length brown hair pushing it out of his eyes.

"We're looking for Sheridan Cunningham," Gabby said.

"Oh, well, okay then. Come on back. You buyers? She's launching a new line you know."

"Friends," Gilly said, arching her brows at Gabby.

"Hey, Sher, you have visitors," Zak shouted.

At the other end of the hallway they stepped into a bright area, the full width of the building, about forty feet and the same depth. Four large windows faced north—light pouring in but no direct sun. Four Mexican looking women, heads bent over their sewing machines, didn't look up to see who had invaded the shop.

On the opposite wall were tacked sketches—twenty-three in all, penned in color, definitely a fall collection of jackets, dresses, skirts and slacks. Two mannequins stood at the far end of two long library tables pushed together. One mannequin was draped in muslin, the other in a cotton print fabric with colorful large red poppies and clusters of green leaves on a white background.

Sheridan's head snapped up from her electronic drawing tablet—eyes wide, slack-jawed. Gilly and Gabby were obviously that last two people she expected to see.

"We were in the area," Gabby said smiling. "Thought we'd drop in."

"Wow! Zak, meet Gilly and Gabby. Friends of mine from Paris." Sheridan rushed to the girls, hugging each in turn, and then stepped back shaking her head.

"Want something to drink? Bottle of water?"

"No, thanks," Gilly said. "We just had lunch. I think we caught you at a bad time. We should have called but—

"Yeah, it is a bad time. We're trying to finish up four samples to show a couple of buyers,"

Zak cut in. "We expect them any minute. Same tomorrow. How about we get together in a couple of days?"

"No. That won't work," Gabby said. "Gilly and I are flying back to Seattle tomorrow."

As Gabby and Sheridan chatted about the possibility of Sheridan rearranging her plans so they could meet for dinner, Gilly walked along the library tables to the mannequin draped in white muslin and then edged her way to the sketches. Scrutinizing the sample with the red poppies on the second mannequin she stole several glances at the sketches tacked to the wall behind the mannequin. She suddenly whirled around, threw her tote on the table and faced Sheridan.

For the second time in less than a few minutes, Sheridan looked startled to see her.

"What the hell are you doing with my designs on your wall?" Gilly yelled.

Gabby immediately strode to the wall to take a look at the renditions.

"I ... I ... I don't know what you're talking about," Sheridan stammered her eyes darting over to Zak.

Gilly whirled back to the wall, stabbed the first print with her index finger. "This is what I'm talking about. My design. And, this one," she yelled stabbing the next picture several times. "And, this, and this, and ... all of them. No wonder you were so shocked to see me. What? You didn't think we'd ever find out you stole my sketches?"

"Ms. Wilder, I wouldn't accuse Ms. Cunningham of stealing your designs," Zak said through clenched teeth. His tone was menacing and the way he squinted, arms across his chest, he appeared ready for a fight.

The four women in the corner conversed in Spanish in loud whispers, fear in their eyes as they scrambled behind their sewing machines, trying to melt into the wall.

Gilly saw them cower. In a quiet voice she snapped at Sheridan. "I see you employ illegals to do your dirty work." She looked from Sheridan to Zak to Gabby. Catching Gabby's eyes shifting to the door, Gilly thought better of another retort. She had seen enough to report Sheridan and her sleazy partner to the police. And, she thought, once back in Seattle she'd sic Hawk on the pair. Scare them. She didn't have the money to bring a lawsuit against them but they didn't know that.

Signaling with her eyes, matching Gabby's, Gilly grabbed her tote off the table and she and Gabby marched down the hallway to the front door.

"I'm really sorry," Sheridan called out. "Keep in touch. Next time you're down this way we definitely have to go out for dinner. No hard feelings. Zak and I will show you around."

Out on the sidewalk the two headed down the street at a fast clip. Gilly, fished her cell out of her tote just as a cab driver exited a drugstore a block away. They ran toward the cab waving their arms. Minutes later they escaped down the street leaving the rundown buildings behind. Gabby gave the driver the name of their hotel and then leaned back in the seat.

Looking straight ahead, both girls alarmed at what they had seen, Gabby said, "If my heart doesn't quit on me before we reach the hotel, remind me never to cross you. You scared me to death. No, let me amend that. You scared me and I was afraid Zak was going to kill both of us. My God, Gilly, you were yelling, of course, you were justified.

Maybe it's your red hair. You brought a whole new meaning to the word HOT back there."

The women still leaning back in the cab, shifted their heads to look at each other now that the orange stucco building was several miles behind them, and their breathing had a semblance of being normal, and smiled.

"Red hair or not, I was steamed," Gilly said. "The nerve. Our entire fall collection on the wall of that crumby, dingy—

"Don't forget smelly," Gabby interjected.

"And smelly place. Did you ever see or suspect that, that dark side of Sheridan?" Gilly said.

"Never. But then I'd never seen your *steamed* side before either," Gabby replied laughing.

In their hotel room, they flopped down on the two queen-sized beds and stared at the ceiling.

"I don't know about you," Gabby said looking over at Gilly. "But I've had enough adventures for one day. How about we order room service. Then we can draw straws as to which one of us gets to tell Nicole about Sheridan."

Gilly threw her pillow at Gabby. "I say I get to tell Nicole about Sheridan and Zak and then you tell Maria and Arthur about FOCUS."

"Man oh man … you never stop. Now you're pulling rank on me," Gabby said reaching for the telephone. "Let's order. I'm starving after my harrowing day with my boss."

Chapter 16

Seattle

Tormented by their visit with Sheridan, Gilly and Gabby climbed the stairs from the shoe shop and entered the loft. Like bees to honey they were immediately swarmed with hugs. Arthur even got into the act and then stepped to the side beaming. He wasn't quite sure what to do with himself but he wasn't going to miss seeing the look on Gilly's face when Maria told her the news.

Nicole and Maria pulled them to the futon then sat Indian style on the floor facing them.

Grinning!

"My God, you two, what happened? Did we win the lottery?" Gilly asked sitting forward laughing at Nicole who couldn't sit still, jumping up from the floor. Then Maria popped up off the floor.

More grins.

"Better than the lottery," Nicole squealed.

"What? What?" Gabby asked. She smiled but didn't know what to make of the pair. Her eyes darted to Arthur who had a permanent smile plastered on his face.

"Gabby …" Maria started to say but paused to catch her breath.

"Yes … go on," Gabby said locking eyes with Gilly. They both shrugged.

"Gabby," Maria continued. "I took a call for you and the woman, Deborah Hollingsworth, would like you to call her back to discuss an order."

"Terrific. A company?" Gabby asked taking a slip of paper from Maria's outstretched hand. She read the name and popped up from the couch, her eyes as big as saucers.

"Gilly, look. Macy's buyer called." Gabby shook the slip of paper in front of Gilly's nose.

Gilly rescued the paper from the shaking fingers and popped up beside Gabby. "Maria, what did she say?"

"Oh, just that one of their buyer's saw your collection at the event last March. They want to include a few pieces in a new display they're adding to their women's department. A special display for the career woman. They are going to begin with twenty, t -w -e -n -t -y, of their major metropolitan stores including … are you ready?"

Nicole couldn't hold it any longer. "New York," she screamed jumping up and down, clapping her hands then grabbed Gilly's arm twirling her around.

All four women were now hugging each other. Arthur slipped away and returned with five plastic water glasses and a bottle of champagne. Grinning, he tried to open the bottle but could only pull down the wire holding the cork. Gabby took the bottle from his shaking hands and did the honor of releasing the cork and poured about an inch of the bubbling contents into the glasses stretched out in front of her. Tapping glasses, Arthur said, "Here's to the beginning of the *national* brand—Gillianne Wilder Fashions."

Gilly closed her eyes, took a sip, and then looked at her team. "Let's expand this little celebration. Maria, do you think Hawk can join us? And, Arthur, how about Cindy? Tell them we're going out for a celebration dinner. Oh, and, Nicole, call Vinsenso. We have to include him."

"I'll do it right now," Nicole giggled. "He's going to faint when he hears."

"Hold on everybody," Gabby said. "Before we go completely crazy, let me call the person at Macy's to be sure she's for real."

Gilly smiled as Nicole stopped running around. "Gabby, you go make that call and then let us know if we're going to dinner down on the waterfront or down the street for a hot dog."

Gabby sat down at the end of the table, her cell phone and the piece of paper with Macy's number in her hands. Arthur corked the champagne bottle and returned it to the refrigerator.

"I'll run down to the shop to make sure our saleslady put the rest of the stock in the proper areas," Nicole said. "Then, Madame Gilly, you have to join us. Inspect the cutest little shop on the street. After all we're opening tomorrow."

"I'll be right down. I have two calls to make first—let Mom know I'll be over to pick up Robyn on Saturday, and, Maria, I have to talk to Hawk. Gabby and I stopped to see Sheridan."

"Oh, how is she? What's the company like?" Nicole asked hesitating at the door and top step to the shoe shop below.

"I'll fill you in later, but right now I'm too furious with our former roommate to give you an answer."

"Oh, oh. Sounds bad," Nicole said.

"It is. She stole our designs. Maria, I can't believe it happened again. First Spiky and now Sheridan. From here on, no one, no one except us five, is allowed in the design studio."

The celebration dinner was on. Gabby confirmed that Deborah Hollingsworth, Macy's buyer, was for real and invited the buyer to visit the shop so Gillianne Wilder could present the collection and what she envisioned for the future of the label.

Boisterous laughter floated throughout the dinner crowd at the Ivar's seafood restaurant. Waiters scooted through the tables holding trays on their shoulders. Trays filled with steaming clam chowder, delicately fried gooey duck clams, baked salmon, as well as sword fish and other seafood favorites. Ivar's seafood restaurant was hopping but none more so than the group seated in the window. The waiter served the Wilder party their second champagne bottle of the day.

They were ready to party—the shop was opening in the morning and they were looking at the prospect of inking a big sale, a sale that would launch GWF nationwide. The little shop in downtown Seattle was going to be its crown jewel, a shop to highlight the Gillianne Wilder Fashion label without distraction from competing brands.

Over coffee, Gilly asked Hawk if they could go for a walk. She had something to discuss with him. Excusing themselves they went outside and walked along the pier behind Ivar's. The June evening had a little nip in the air and Gilly pulled on her sweater as she began relating her confrontation with Sheridan Cunningham. "I feel so stupid that I let my guard down … again."

"You're doing the right thing … closing off the studio to everyone but you and your staff," Hawk said leaning on a piling sticking up out of the water anchoring a chain to the next piling. "If you have to meet with someone, get together down in Gabby's sales area in the back of the shop. Besides with the renovation, her sales space is beautiful, and, if the appointment calls for a more personal touch, you can meet in the living room of your new apartment when its ready." Hawk paused, then looked with a furrowed brow at Gilly. "You have to remember your studio is like a company's R&D laboratory. It holds the current and future designs of the GWF label. Another thing, when a design is ready to be sampled in muslin, bring it to me and I'll immediately register the copyright."

"You're right, Hawk. I guess the horse is out of the barn as far as Sheridan is concerned," Gilly said looking out over the water. A full moon provided cascading beams of light over the rippling tidal water.

"Well, yes, but that doesn't mean we can't scare her, maybe enough so she'll abandon the idea of using your designs. I'll write a letter, as your lawyer, saying you are going to sue her, her partner, and her company for the theft of your designs. We won't actually sue but they won't know that—get them looking over their shoulder worrying about what's coming. And there's one more thing I'll do."

"What's that?" Gilly smiled at her long-time friend. How lucky she was to have him and how lucky he married Maria, keeping them in a tight-knit group.

"Maria and I have been talking about going to San Francisco for a few days, and I'm sure I can talk her into visiting Los Angeles as well. Maybe we'll duck out early next week. With the shop opening tomorrow, I'm sure she'll be ready for a little pampering."

"And, my friend, you're just the guy to handle that assignment. Thanks, Hawk. Let me know what you think of my conniving former friend in LA."

Chapter 17

Los Angeles

An American Indian dressed in a black suit, tie, and white silk shirt, stepped out of the cab and frowned at the rundown orange stucco building in front of him. With a sigh he stepped through the door of a shop with a smudged display window and faced a counter, a dingy empty space, and no one in attendance. Exactly as it had been described to him.

"Hey. Anyone here," he yelled. "Hey—"

"Yeah. Yeah. Keep your britches on," a voice hollered from the hallway. A man emerged with a can of beer in his hand.

Bingo, the Indian thought—baggy jeans, scuffed sneakers, and Zak stitched on a tank top—my man.

"What you want, mister?" the man in the shirt named Zak said setting his beer on the counter and swiping hair out of his eyes.

The visitor looked around, frowned. "I must be in the wrong place. Looking for a designer by the name of Sheridan Cunningham."

"You've come to the right place. You a buyer?"

"Maybe."

"Well, it's a pleasure to meet you. My names Zak, Zak Foster, mister?"

"Hawk Jackson." His black hair was slicked back into a short pony tail.

"Well, you come with me, Mr. Jackson. Ms. Cunningham is in the back ... in her studio. You've come at a good time. She's finishing up her designs for a new collection. A fall collection," Zak said leading the way through the shadowy hall and into a bright, large room.

Hawk glanced at the Mexican women pushing fabric under the foot of the sewing machines, the needle pounding as they pushed. Three women today.

"Sheridan, this is Mr. Jackson, a buyer. He heard about your designs."

"Welcome, Mr. Jackson." Sheridan smiled extending her hand. "Anything in particular you're looking for?"

"Yes. My fall line needs a fresh look. I heard from an attendant preparing for the LA Fashion Week in October that you were working on a new line. Spring collections of course will be shown in October, but I was hoping to buy some items now for fall. May I see your collection?"

"Yes. However, I only have the sketches at the moment. The patterns are being cut elsewhere, and the muslin samples aren't complete. But, come over here and I'll show you the sketches. If there is anything you like, I'm sure we could quickly fill your order." Sheridan walked to the sketches tacked to the fall.

"Take a look at these—the complete fall collection."

Hawk stepped to the first sketch, paused, stepped back, stepped to the next. "Do you have fabric samples?"

"Expect the bolts of fabric to be delivered in a few days. I can describe the weave, the blends—

"That's all right. I like your work, Miss Cunningham. It is Miss Cunningham?"

"Yes. Zak is my business partner."

Zak rocked on his feet, a slight nod, at the mention of his name. His hands folded behind his back.

"I have to make a call ... to my corporate office." Hawk patted his jack pocket, his breast pocket, both pants pockets. "I seem to have left my cell phone at the hotel. Could I borrow yours, Miss Cunningham?"

"Of course." Sheridan picked up her cell from the table and handed it to Hawk.

"Thank you. If you don't mind I'll just step out front a minute ... easier to talk," he said winking at Sheridan. He turned and started down the hall, catching the pair high-fiving out of the corner of his eye.

At the front counter he quickly activated the phone, tapped the picture icon and flipped through the frames. Satisfied that most, if not all of Gilly's sketches were still stored on the phone, he smiled. Yes, he thought, this will give her a nice piece of insurance against Sheridan ever daring to use the designs.

Hawk pocketed the phone and left, climbing into his waiting cab.

Hearing the front door bang shut, Sheridan ran down the hall. "Hey, where are you going? My phone." She ran out into the street, Zak on her heels. "Hey, mister, my phone," she hollered to the cab speeding away. "Give me my goddamn phone."

Hawk looked out the back window. Their high-fives had turned into very obscene gestures.

Chapter 18

Hansville

Breath in. Breath out.

"In. In.

"Out. Out."

Running at a slow pace, Skip kept his breathing in cadence with his stride. Two strides: inhale. Two strides: exhale. His second pair of new shoes felt good. He had to replace the first pair since they didn't leave the suggested inch between his big toe and the shoe leather for distance running. Knee length shorts were just right—no friction between the thighs. His neck and shoulders were relaxed.

"I see myself running easily. I feel strong, I feel powerful. I can run forever." His mantra. Today he said the words out loud, then let them run through his head several times. As important as getting his muscles and bones hardened, was setting the mental images. He had to maintain a positive attitude—all part of marathon training.

His goal was to finish. It didn't matter how long it took, as long as he finished.

Four more weeks and he would start the sixteen-week training program his college coach had given to all students who had signed up to run a marathon—26.2 miles. Running the marathon was at the end of the fifteenth week. Week sixteen was recovery, refortifying what was depleted during the rigors of the race. The preliminary training was not for speed or endurance, but to run slow and easy in preparation for the longer distances to come. Today was Saturday—a long run of four miles.

He focused once again on his breathing pattern: breathe in for two strides and breathe out for two strides.

"In. In."

"Out. Out."

The same motorcycle that passed him last Saturday pulled around him again this morning. The man, with a girl straddling the seat behind, waved as they passed.

"Stay positive. Looks like rain ... but it doesn't matter. There's a hill ahead ... but it doesn't matter." Skip smiled. He remembered how he hated hills but then his coach told him if there is something you don't like, say to yourself *but it doesn't matter* and let it go. The first day after being given those words he saw a huge hill ahead. He had laughed out loud ... "but, it doesn't matter," and took the hill in stride.

"In. In."

"Out. Out."

The Eglon sign was ahead, he ran up to the marker, tapped it, turned around and without breaking stride headed back to Gramp's house.

Approaching the driveway he saw two cars parked next to his Jeep. One was Gilly's, the other her mom's. His concentration broke and then his stride. Breathing turned erratic. His heart rate spiked, a smile spreading across his face. Gilly was here.

He trotted down the steps to the patio door, swung it open and called out, "Hey, where is everybody?"

"In the kitchen, son," Gramp's called back.

The three were sitting at the kitchen table sharing a cup of tea. Skip was so happy to see them, he kissed Anne and then Gilly on the cheek.

"Gramps tells me you're taking up residence on the weekends—the two Rs," Gilly said

"Two Rs? What's that supposed to mean?" Skip asked rinsing the empty water bottle on his belt, refilling it, and draining half.

"Running and wRiting," she said with a giggle throwing him a hand towel to wipe the water dripping from the stubble on his chin.

"Cute," he replied with a smirk. "How about a walk on the beach, smarty pants? It's a beautiful day—first of July. The fourth coming up."

"Thanks, for the invite, but I was just about to leave."

"Nonsense," Gramps said. "There's always another ferry."

"Go ahead," Anne said. "Robyn's still sleeping."

"Well, in that case, the last one on the beach is a snarky turtle," Gilly said as she ran down the hall, out the patio door, skidding to a halt at the top of the rickety stairs.

Skip caught up with her and they disappeared down over the bank.

"How far did you run today?" Gilly asked dropping from the bottom rung of the ladder to the beach. The tide was out leaving a mixture of small rocks and sand as well as streamers of bright green slimy kelp releasing the smell of seaweed.

"Four miles. Not far. Still in the preliminary phase of my training—toughening up the muscles and bones," he said joining her.

"Ah, your bones are talking to you again." They both laughed thinking back to the time he was the first reporter on the scene when a body was found on the Hansville beach. He had said his bones told him the man was murdered. "Could feel it in my bones" were his exact words.

"And your exposé, how's it coming along?" Gilly asked shading her eyes from the brilliant noon sun.

"I still have a couple more chapters to write. Eleanor's trial won't happen for several months, maybe not until the first of the year, but I'm not going to wait for the verdict. I doubt she'll get the death penalty given there's no body. At least that's what DuBois says. So, I'll write the ending that she's hit with a life sentence. The main thing is we know she helped Sacco over the railing."

"By the time an agent hooks you up with a publisher you'll probably know the actual sentence—change a few words."

"Don't even mention the words agent and publisher. I'll have three or more books written before that happens."

Gilly stopped walking and looked into Skip's intense blue eyes. "I'm so happy to hear you talk like that. And, I'm a little jealous that you're out here on weekends with Gramps … writing."

"He's terrific. We don't talk much except at dinner. I asked him how the deck was named the Queen Betty."

"And he said that—

"He said that when you were a little girl, on Sunday morning he and your Grandmother Betty served blueberry pancakes for breakfast down on the deck. And, that your dad dubbed the deck the Queen Betty. Right?"

"Right. Breakfast on the Queen Betty. It was wonderful." Gilly dug the toe of her shoe in the rocky sand.

"Now that I'm in training," Skip said in a stern voice, "Your grandfather is asking me for a list of food I should be eating. Then he buys the stuff during the week. And then there's your mom. Holy cow, does she ever stop cooking?"

"Never!" Gilly laughed. "So what are you supposed to eat?"

"Lots of carbs like oatmeal and pasta, which I love, and vegetables, which I'm growing to love. I never knew broccoli could be cooked so many different ways."

"Umm, Mom has a million pasta recipes. Some with broccoli as I recall."

"And then there's protein—fish, chicken, beans, nuts, whole grains, egg whites, low-fat milk, low-fat cheese and—

"Stop. You're making me hungry."

Skip looked at her smiling face turned up to him. He threw caution to the wind, grasped her shoulders and pulled her into his arms, and tenderly kissed her pink lips. Releasing her, he started to jog up the beach. "Come on. Let's run up to that boulder."

Gilly stood rooted to the ground, smiling, but shaking her head, no. He walked back. "Okay, but what about next Saturday? Come over and help me eat Gramp's banquet."

"I don't think I can. I'm only here today because Mom took care of Robyn for a few days. We're crazy busy now that the shop has reopened. Stop over, or run over when you get a chance."

"I'll do that." He held her hand as they walked back to the rickety stairs.

If they had been looking up at the top of the bank several houses down, they would have caught a flash of light through a cluster of bushes, the sun's rays reflecting off the lens of a pair of binoculars. The binoculars were trained on the pair down on the beach as they approached a flight of rickety stairs.

Chapter 19

Paris

Summer flowers filled the sidewalk stalls along the Avenue des Champs-Élysées. Tourists filled the outdoor cafes and double-decker sightseeing buses. Vehicles of all sizes jammed the streets jockeying for position, an opening to make a dash to their destination. The aroma of coffee mixed with the scent of roses mingled with the exhaust of the busses. All in all it was a thrilling weekend in the city of love.

Maxime gazed out of his luxury apartment window at the gently flowing waters of the Seine twinkling in the sunlight. He had made some decisions since returning from Seattle, the image of Gillianne cradling their baby seared into his brain. He knew the chance of winning her heart again was very, very, remote. But no matter how remote he had to try. And, he had to get his life back, a life that had slipped off the tracks. Too much deference to his mother and father, especially his father.

Adding up the plusses and minuses, he had to give his parents credit for providing him a pathway to join the family law practice. With his family's connections he had had no trouble in gaining admittance to the University of Paris 1 Panthéon-Sorbonne which offered a top level degree in law and political science. He had soaked up every word his professors uttered. He had a passion for the law, had enthusiastically embraced his studies, and had finished in the top five of his class.

Now practicing law in the firm his grandfather founded and being elected to the Senate, the career side of his life's ledger was in good order.

Ah, but his personal life was another matter. It was in tatters. He had entered a loveless marriage to please his parents, and regrettably he had remained in the marriage. But the worst part, he had bungled the opportunity to grasp the love of his life. How stupid could a man be?

He wasn't sure if he would ever be able to regain Gillianne's trust but in order to begin the process of restoring his personal life, putting it back on the right track, he had to deal with Bernadette.

It was time.

Way past time.

Maxime pressed the intercom button for Eric, his valet, and asked him to tell Bernadette he wanted to talk to her and to bring their afternoon cocktails to his library.

The cocktails arrived before Bernadette, and Maxime poured his martini from the decanter into his glass. Bernadette entered the room as Maxime took his first sip.

"Maxime, we're starting a little early aren't we? We're not due to arrive at your father's for another two hours," she said. Maxime was standing at the other side of the library, a room encased in walnut bookcases filled with law books, filled with the musty fragrance of history. Bernadette hated this room—hundreds of books none of which interested her in the slightest. His back was to her as he had taken up his position at the window. He did not address her question.

She helped herself to a martini and a salmon canapé, and then sat uncomfortably in a brown leather chair sinking into the generous cushion. "Did you have something you wanted to discuss? If it's about that dreadful—

"I've called my father and cancelled our dinner plans."

"You what?" Bernadette snapped. "We always have dinner with the Count on Saturday night. What's the matter with you? Are you trying to pick a fight with him? Or maybe you're trying to pick a fight with me. Why aren't we going—

Maxime turned around. Stared at his pinched-face wife. Some would say she was beautiful, he thought. But her greed for money, and her snarly attitude had lined her face and had taken away any warmth and compassion that might have been there at one time. However, Maxime now believed love was never there only an evil plan to ingratiate her way into his life.

"I've drawn up divorce papers." Maxime strode to his desk, picked up a manila envelope and handed it to Bernadette. Standing near her, her perfume filled his nostrils—heavy, overwhelmingly sweet. How he detested the smell of her.

Bernadette did not reach for the envelope. Instead she took a sip of her cocktail letting the envelope drop to her lap.

"Maxime, what we need to fix our marriage is a child. A baby to love, and then we will learn to love each other in return."

"Bernadette, we never loved each other, AND it would be wrong to bring a child into this loveless union. Take the envelope, look over the papers. I think you will see I've been quite generous—our villa in southern France along with a generous allowance. It may not be the amount you are used to spending, but more than enough to staff the villa and generous enough so that you will be able to have a nice, worry-free life style unless you choose to squander the money."

Bernadette drained her drink and smiled coyly at Maxime's back. "Mark my words, a child will make all the difference in the world, my dear husband."

Maxime turned. His eyes full of hate. "Take the papers. Hire your own attorney. He'll tell you to take the offer and be quick about it. However you want to handle your side is up to you. The signed papers are to be back in my hand by mid August. Do you understand?"

"Perfectly, Senator."

"Good. You are to be out of this apartment by the end of next week. If you are not your rooms will be packed and moved to the villa for you."

Bernadette put her empty glass on the silver tray and left the room clutching the envelope, her jaw clenched, her breathing rapid and shallow."

Maxime quickened his steps as he left his apartment building emerging into the morning sunshine. How grand a day it is, he thought. The weight of ten years of a loveless marriage had been lifted from his shoulders. Giving Bernadette the divorce papers had gone rather smoothly. At least she hadn't thrown a tirade, or thrown a glass at him, only repeating that a child would solve all their woes.

Tourists smiled back at the handsome Frenchman who smiled at everyone he passed, nodding his head over and over again in greeting.

During the night he had thought of going on a little shopping spree—pink baby clothes for Robyn. A frilly little dress, cute bunny pajamas—surely the baby shop down the block would be able to help him.

Two hours later, four bags with handles swinging by his side, he stopped at an outdoor café a few blocks from his building and ordered an espresso. Smiling, he once again looked out over the Seine and asked the waiter for a piece of paper with the café's name on it. He and Gillianne had stopped here once. Maybe she would remember it. The waiter returned quickly with a piece of stationery, refreshed the coffee, and hustled to the next table.

Maxime retrieved a pen from his pocket and wrote a short note to Gillianne telling her he couldn't resist buying the enclosed gifts for Robyn. He told her the saleslady urged him to buy sizes for a one year old—"they grow so fast she said. I didn't listen to her. Our baby is so tiny that I purchased everything marked *six months*." He signed the note, "*Your Maxime*."

Back home, he asked Eric to bring him a box sturdy enough for shipment to Seattle, in America. Carefully laying each item, wrapped in white tissue, into the box, he folded the note he had written, put it in an envelope with the seal of the French Senate in the upper left corner, and placed it on the top layer of tissue paper. He addressed the box to Gillianne Wilder at her little shop. He wrote at an angle next to the address: Open by Addressee Only.

Chapter 20

Seattle

Paintings of the Montana mountains and plateaus, as well as framed photographs of his herd of black angus cattle filled the walls of the long hallway from the front door to Philip Wellington's library. Sauntering along the gallery beside Gillianne, Philip explained to her, through the artwork, his love for his ranch—the beauty of the land but also the hard work the ranch demanded of his life.

"Do you miss your ranch, Mr. Wellington?"

"Oh dear, you called me Mr. Wellington again. This visit must be serious," he said pulling his face into a mock squint.

Gilly laughed. "You win, Philip. I asked to see you because I have a business proposition." Her lips parted in a radiant smile, green eyes sparkling.

"Oh, good. Most people coming to me with a business proposition," he said in a stern voice pulling his chin into his chest, "Are stodgy old men. Finally, a delightful, beautiful woman once again lights up my home. Have a seat, Gilly. If we're going to talk business we must have coffee." He pushed a button on the intercom. "Gladys, please bring a coffee service to the library for Gilly and myself and put some of that seed concoction on the tray that Skip Hunter dropped off the other day. Thanks."

Gilly removed her black suit jacket, laying it on the back of the caramel-colored leather couch. Smoothing her black skirt and white short-sleeved blouse, she sat down facing Philip over a coffee table. A table carved from a large round section of a ponderosa pine, the official state tree of Montana, another piece of nostalgia from his ranch.

"So, Skip gave you some of his seed mixture. He must have told you he's training to run in the Seattle marathon."

"Can you believe it?" Philip said, nodding to Gladys as she set the silver tray on the highly polished coffee table.

"How's that baby, Ms. Wilder?" Gladys asked her rosy cheeks and pink lips drawn into a broad smile.

"Growing like a weed, Gladys."

"Can you bring her by sometime? We'd love to see that little darling."

"You bet I can."

Gladys beamed and then left returning to her household duties humming softly.

Philip lifted a crystal bowl of seeds offering them to Gilly. She picked up a few, put them in the palm of her hand and then poured coffee into their cups.

"Skip and Agatha … have you met Agatha?" Gilly asked.

"Oh, yes. That dog of his is a real character."

"She sure is. Anyway, he and Agatha visit Gramps every Saturday for his long training run. Then they kibitz over lunch. Skip writes the rest of the day and most of Sunday, and then returns to the city."

"Your grandfather must love that … the company."

Gilly smiled popping a couple of the seeds into her mouth.

"Now, tell me about this proposition, young lady, and don't skimp on the details." Philip smiled enjoying his visitor.

"Well, so much has happened in the last few months. I don't know if you've passed my shop lately, but—

"Yes, I have. You've reopened and it looks charming—from the outside mind you. How about the second floor loft? Ready for you soon, I hope."

"Actually, next week." Gilly helped herself to a cashew. "A few weeks ago, Gabby and I went to LA to check out the site of their fashion week next March. I'm taking my staff to LA to see the fall show to observe the event in action—see what works and what doesn't, and how best to present our collection. We'll also pick up information from the models, their agencies, and the hair and makeup stylists."

"Sounds like a big deal," Philip said leaning back in the couch across from Gilly.

"Oh, it is. IMG sponsors—"

"What is IMG? Never heard of them," Philip asked.

"IMG stands for International Marketing Group. They sponsor all kinds of sporting and media events. They also sponsor the New York Fashion Week along with Mercedes Benz. Same for the LA show."

"When is the LA show? You said the fall?"

"October, but we're just going to observe. We're signed up for the March show. But, listen to this, when Gabby and I returned to Seattle, after our first trip to LA, Nicole and Maria were literally bouncing off the walls."

Philip smiled. Gilly's enthusiasm was contagious. He leaned forward elbows on his knees so as not to miss a single nuance of what she was saying.

"They took a call from Macy's ... New York, no less, wanting to place an order for our fall collection ...*for several of their biggest stores! And*, that's why I'm here."

"Go on."

"Well ..."

"Let it out, Gilly, before you burst. Tell me why you're here. Your proposal," Philip said chuckling, urging her on.

Gilly inhaled a deep breath. "I need $200,000—some to participate in the show but at least eighty percent would go to start filling the orders for Macy's. They're paying a deposit but it won't cover the factory costs to fill the orders, let alone the fabric."

There she said it. What's he thinking, she wondered? He's laughing. Why is he laughing? Did I mix up my words?

"Oh, my goodness. You are a treat. The way you were leading up to the money ... it's always about the money you know ... business. I was expecting you to ask me for a million. So, now tell me, what do I get for $200,000?"

"My lawyer, you met him, Hawk Jackson. He and Maria are married. Anyway, Hawk set up my business as a corporation. I asked him and my accountant, Arthur Lewis, whom you also met, to let me know how an investor might benefit. The long and short of it is that you will own a share of the company. Hawk and Arthur will explain how that works."

"Oh, I know how that works—the number of shares, the actual percentage of the company the investment will represent. They'll spell it out for me I'm sure. I only have one question."

"What's that, Philip? Of course, we, I will work very hard to be sure you don't lose your investment, that—

"Lose my investment?" Again he laughed. "I've seen you in action Ms. Gillianne Wilder. The morning of the fire, the way you took hold. No fire was going to stop you. I saw so much of myself struggling those first years with my ranch, struggling against all kinds of odds—droughts, falling prices of beef. The money is yours, my dear. My question is about the amount."

"If I'm asking for too much—

"No, it's not too much. My question—is it enough?"

Chapter 21

Everything was clean, fresh. The heavy odor of refinished oak floors was long gone, and the stink of new construction, spackled wallboard, and freshly painted cream walls had dissipated. Only the smell of *new* remained in the air.

The *Band of 5*, Arthur's nickname for the four women and one male, made quick work moving from the loft above the shoe and mobile phone stores to the loft over Gillianne Wilder Fashions, *Catering to the Career Woman*. All the rented furnishings were picked up ending that expense, but the lease for the restored building kicked in—the landlord giving the fledging business one month free.

Thanks to Maria's and Gabby's constant efforts to build excitement for the reopening of the shop, they had created a buzz as pedestrians consistently lined up at the display windows to catch the activity going on inside—the transformation from smoked filled, damaged interior to a showcase for the summer collection. A splash of color and sophistication was revealed in the display windows when the glass door swung open for business three weeks earlier.

The loft apartment featured three small bedrooms, a bath—one side for bathing the other a long vanity with mirror—enough space to handle two women applying makeup or drying their hair at the same time.

Gilly's bedroom was larger than the other two providing an alcove for Robyn, giving Nicole and Gabby their own bedrooms. Nicole hadn't had the luxury of her own bedroom since leaving home to work in Paris over three years ago.

The living room, a *great room* in some homes, was an open space separated by an island in the back corner concealing a galley kitchen—sleek, modern, and small, but efficient enough to prepare spaghetti, or zap a frozen dinner—no gourmet meals allowed. Furniture was still an issue, non-existent, as the pieces they had accumulated were all destroyed in the fire. However, Maria and Hawk gave Gilly a bedroom set—bed, nightstand, and dresser; Nicole's parents sent her a check—enough for a bed and dresser; and Gabby purchased a bed but stacked boxes on end as makeshift shelving until she found a dresser.

Anne and Gramps found a couch, practically new, at a garage sale along with four barstools perfect for eating at the island counter. Skip sauntered in with two of his reporter friends carrying an eight-by-ten foot oriental rug from a discount warehouse—they rolled it out anchoring the great room. Gilly returned to the used furniture shop where she had purchased the furnishings for her baby before Robyn was born and bought a couple of items to fill in what was still needed—absolutely needed.

Home!

The design studio was separated from the front of the loft by a wall and three doors—an exit to the back ally, an entrance to the apartment, and an entrance to the small hallway at the top of the center staircase to the shop below. The studio was painted a soft, creamy white separated by large windows at the back providing natural northern light. Three strips of track lighting ran across the beamed ceiling. Two eight-foot folding tables were in the center of the room with five black metal folding chairs, padded seats. Another three were leaning against the wall.

The studio was Gilly's bailiwick. Two mannequins stood guard over the space and once again Will, her dad, provided the muscles, along with Arthur in hanging a whiteboard, and two eight-foot sections of corkboard to tack printouts of the latest collection as it evolved. A few bolts of fabric leaned against the wall in the corner, more were on the way from the factory—Vinsenso and Nicole had sourced new stretchy wool from a supplier as well as new silk blends, and a few bolts of holiday fabrics Gilly had requested.

Arthur commandeered a corner—a desk, file cabinet, and a small four-foot table.

Gabby's client area in the back of the shop had already been set up before the shop reopened. The furnishings included a glass coffee table, two upholstered chairs, and a loveseat. The upholstered pieces using the same black on white fabric as the white lacquered chairs in the shop—striped cushions set against fabric of toile French scenes—tufted back and arms. After seeing Skip's gift, Gabby visited the same warehouse and purchased a burgundy, five-foot oval Aubusson rug. The area to greet buyers, or a customer who wanted to order pieces of the collection that were not currently in stock, was charming and the rug grounded the little business space with class.

At the end of the day, the move complete, Hawk dropped in to take a peek at the new digs and insisted that the *Band of 5* relax over dinner and drinks at Ivar's, their favorite restaurant, on the waterfront—his treat. The group was well known and even had a waiter assigned to their table when any, or all, of the Band of 5 came into the establishment.

It was six o'clock, closing time, so Gilly went down the stairs, said goodbye and thanks to the young saleswoman, and locked the front door. A carton about one foot in diameter was on the floor in back of the glass sales counter. *Gillianne Wilder, Open by Addressee Only.* Gilly's heart skipped a beat. The return address: Maxime Beaumont. She stared at the box for a moment and decided to open it when she returned. Dinner with the Band of 5 was not going to be ruined by whatever was in the box.

She hurried back upstairs, dressed Robyn in a playsuit with a sweater knotted around the baby's shoulders. "You look very chic, my chérie," Gilly laughed. Now five-and-a half months old Robyn was sitting in her crib, holding a cracker, laughing and babbling—an adorable moppet with red curls spilling around her face. Her dark eyes followed anything moving in her line of sight.

———◇———

Dinner was lively. Thanks to Maria and Hawk, it was just what the Band of 5 needed. Hawk had graciously whispered to Arthur to ask Cindy to join them. After one glass of wine with dinner, the Band of 5 began to wilt. The long day of moving accompanied with the excitement to finally combine the loft with the shop, had taken its toll. Skipping dessert and passing on an after dinner coffee, they straggled out of the restaurant. Their only words: "Bye, see you tomorrow."

Gilly drove Nicole, Gabby, and Robyn back to the apartment—the first night in their new home. It was like old times—the three friends laughing and giggling as they mounted the stairs and stepped into the apartment. They stood gazing around the great room, without saying a word they gave each other a high five and headed to their separate bedrooms—what luxury.

Gilly changed Robyn into her pajamas, covered her with a light baby blanket and kissed her forehead. Her eyes closed instantly. She had been the life of the party and was exhausted with all the tummy tickles from her five mothers. Gilly tiptoed to her dresser, the only illumination in the room from a small lamp on the nightstand. Looking into the mirror she removed her earrings. An image of Maxime flashed into her mind. Why in the world am I thinking of him, she wondered frowning. Then she remembered the box downstairs.

She crept down to the shop and lifted the box—it was light. She crept back up the stairs to her bedroom and closed the door. Slitting the tape with a nail file, she opened the box revealing white tissue paper with an envelope on top. Removing the note, she let out a small sigh shaking her head—"Your Maxime," written by his hand at the bottom.

Setting the note on her dresser she pulled the tissue paper away, her lips drawing into a smile, her green eyes crinkling at the corners as she unwrapped a frilly little pink dress, a yellow T-shirt with a painted bunny in the center, little white patent shoes, frilly socks, a white sweater with pearl buttons, a pink barrette, and a little white bunny with a pink satin ribbon around his neck tied in a bow.

Still smiling, she kissed the bunny and tiptoed to her sleeping baby, tucking the bunny under Robyn's arm. A fuzzy ear brushed the infant's cheek. Her little hand swiped in the air at the tickle and then her arm circled the bunny pulling it to her heart. Witnessing the move Gilly gulped for air, her eyes misting as she stared at the picture in front of her. On tiptoe, she ran from the alcove and the sleeping child, stuffed the tissue back into the box and put it by the door. Returning to her bed, she quickly folded each piece of clothing, stacking them in the bottom drawer of her dresser.

Changing into a green shorty gown, she crawled under the new, cool sheets, reached for the lamp and turned off the light. Her eyes wide, she played over opening the box, the note, the adorable outfits, and then Robyn's grasp of the bunny. Why, she wondered, didn't I return the box unopened to the sender?

Exhausted from the emotions of the day, her eyes fluttered and she fell into a deep, peaceful sleep.

Chapter 22

The newsroom was abuzz over a plane performing an emergency landing with eighty-three passengers aboard at SeaTac airport. It was Friday, quitting time, and Skip was about to make a quick exit before he was called to a crime scene. An emergency landing of a plane didn't qualify as a crime, not at the moment anyway. He powered down his computer, grabbed his jacket from the wall peg and bumped into Diane as she turned into his cubicle.

"Hey, Skipper, how about a TGIF beer at Charlie's?"

"Sorry, Di, no can do. I'm on way home to pick up Agatha and then heading across the sound."

"Oh, yeah, I forgot your Saturday morning training run. How's it going?"

"Great. Tomorrow's August fourteenth—the beginning of week two."

"Two?"

"My second week of the training program—fifteen being the marathon and then one to recoup. See you Monday," he called over his shoulder.

Diane exhaled a long sigh, hands on her hips. "Maybe I should run a marathon, or help you recoup," she called after him.

"Try it. It's a lot of fun," he yelled back and stopped. Turning around he looked at her, her arms crossed over her chest, standing with a sour look on her face. "But, it's also a lot of work. Bye."

Two hours later Skip pulled into Gramp's driveway, beeped the horn and let a restless hound out of the Jeep. Agatha bumped down the stairs to the patio waiting for Gramp's to open the screen door.

"Hello there, my furry friend," Gramps said opening the door. Agatha scooted past him and straight to the doorway between the living room and kitchen—the spot gramps had taken to laying a rawhide bone when he expected her to visit. Aggie whizzed by a hissing Coco. Gramps was laughing as Skip passed him on his way to the den, arms around his laptop and a box of papers and folders for his weekend writing session. He set everything on the desk and then stripped off his trousers and shirt revealing his running clothes—red long shorts and a yellow tank. He looked like a big stop light which was exactly his intent.

"See you later—six miles today," he called out as he jogged to the driveway to stretch for five minutes before starting his run.

"Gilly called from the ferry," Gramps shouted as he pulled the lounger for Gilly from the patio. "She asked me to set up the playpen on the lawn with a chair umbrella attached to the rail to protect Robyn from the sun. She may pass you."

"Need some help?" Skip shouted back.

Gramps shook his head, no, returning inside the patio for the playpen and umbrella.

Finished stretching, Skip downed a bottle of water and stashed another in his backpack along with a Gatorade, a key carbohydrate and sodium replacement drink on a hot day like today. He picked up his watch, looked at it a minute and then put it back in his bag. Time didn't matter—his goal was to finish. He didn't want the distraction of checking his watch.

One more stretch and then he jogged up the driveway and turned south on Hansville Road. "I feel good. I'm a marathoner," he said with a grin. He had gradually allowed his muscular and skeletal system to adapt to the trauma of running.

"In. In.

"Out. Out

"In. In.

"Out. Out"

He focused on his running form, especially his lower body. Focused on his foot striking the pavement—heel first. Some runners made contact with the heel and forefoot at the same time. Heel first came naturally to Skip, so he didn't try to change.

"In. In.
"Out. Out
"In. In.
"Out. Out"

He focused on his vertical bounce, making sure it wasn't excessive—a waste of energy. He focused on his upper body. A slight lean forward, neck and shoulders relaxed, arms bent. Ninety degrees or a little more was his comfort zone, breathing with his mouth open, the air entering his lungs from both his nose and mouth.

"In. In.
"Out. Out
"In. In.
"Out. Out"

Man, it's getting hot, he thought. He smiled and shouted his mantra to a cow in the field as he passed. "But it doesn't matter."

He pulled his bottle of Gatorade from his pack, drank half, and returned the bottle to his pack. Walked a minute then started running again. The motorcycle with the man and woman, same as the last few weeks, passed but didn't wave this time.

He thought about his training week. He had begun to drink more water, ate more veggies, kept to low-fat foods. Monday he ran three miles, Tuesday four, Thursday three, today six. He totaled sixteen miles for the week. Right on schedule.

"In. In.
"Out. Out

Gilly drove by. Honked. Waved.

Skip waved. Focused back on the pavement a few yards ahead.

Chapter 23

Gilly drove with the windows up to thwart the blast of hot air, the AC on high as she crested the hill then dropping into Hansville, Puget Sound lying out in front of her. A quarter mile farther she turned down Gramp's driveway and parked next to Skip's Jeep.

Lifting Robyn from her car seat, she carefully navigated the three steps to the lawn and put Robyn in the playpen. Gramps came to the door to greet his granddaughter, kissed her on the cheek and smiled at his great granddaughter.

"Thanks for putting up the playpen, Gramps. I passed Skip so I should have time to bask in the sun for a while before putting Robyn down for her nap."

"Your mother brought over a fish stew earlier."

"Fish?"

"Yes, she's been reading up on diets for marathoners. Seems fish was near the top of the list," he chuckled and ducked inside out of the heat.

Gilly kicked off her sandals, handed Robyn her *now* favorite toy—the white bunny—and settled herself on the lounger. She tied the shirttails of her blouse in a knot above her white shorts. It was a peaceful summer afternoon and it felt good to be away from the shop for a few hours.

Shielding her eyes she gazed at Gramp's garden from the guesthouse up to the road. Her eyes lingered over the strip of grass from the garage to the berry bushes, the round bed of roses in the middle, the pine trees marching up the side of the driveway and opposite the large flowering bushes up the other side. The far end, shielding the road, was a big raspberry and blackberry patch. Something caught her eye through the leaves in the blackberry patch. She propped herself up on her elbows but didn't see anything moving. Probably just the leaves fluttering in the breeze, she thought, or some squirrels playing tag. She looked over at Robyn swatting a toy fastened to the side of the playpen, and then she lay back reveling in the heat of the sun's rays on her skin.

Hearing a car slowly roll down the driveway, Gilly lifted her head, her hand raised to her forehead protecting her eyes from the sun as the car parked behind Skip's Jeep.

Helen Churchill emerged from the car a few seconds later and stood at the top of the steps her face hardened in a frown.

"Helen, hi. Nice to see you," Gilly said, squirming to get up from the lounger. "Come on down. See how Robyn's grown."

"Stay where you are, Gillianne Wilder," Helen snapped.

Gilly was startled at the guttural sound of Helen's voice. She took a step away from the lounger and another toward Helen, who was still standing on the edge of the driveway.

"I said, stay where you are," Helen yelled. She pulled something from her tote, one of Gilly's totes the woman had purchased at the Port Gamble Boutique.

Gilly, blinded by the sun, couldn't see what was in Helen's hand. It was shiny and caught a glint from the sunlight.

Gilly took another step.

Helen was holding a pistol.

She was pointing it at Gilly.

Gramps opened the screen door. Gilly waved her hand behind her warding him off but he walked up beside her to say hello to his friend.

"Helen, how are—

"Stay where you are Clayton Wilder. I'll tell you both how I am. I'm sick with grief." Tears sprang from her eyes.

"Helen, what's the matter? And please put that gun away. Talk to us," Gramps said taking a step toward her.

"The matter? Edward's dead. You killed him ... both of you. Well, let's see how it feels to take a bullet in the foot Mr. Clay Wilder."

Helen pulled the trigger. The bullet flew up in the air the recoil throwing Helen off balance, her shoulder banging into the side of the guesthouse. Huffing, putting her hand against the clapboards, she struggled to regain her footing.

"What happened to your grandson, Helen?" Gramps asked in a low voice inching forward.

"In prison, thanks to you. He was bullied and beaten. Last night they found him in his cell. Dead," she said dazed then quickly focusing again on Gilly and Gramps.

Gilly knew Skip would not return in time to help. She and Gramps had to somehow talk Helen into giving up the gun. She glanced sideways at her grandfather. He was holding his hands out, open to Helen, showing her he was not a threat.

"It's your fault," Helen screamed at him. "If you hadn't shot him, if the police hadn't chased him for no good reason ... he didn't copy your designs, Miss Gillianne Wilder," she hissed. She waggled the gun at Gramps. "If you hadn't shot him, hurt him ... he was in such pain ... he wouldn't have gone to Mexico. They butchered his leg. All your fault," she said hatred burning in her eyes.

The pistol fired. Again she was thrown off balance from the recoil. The bullet penetrated the patio window leaving a hole and cracked glass.

Helen suddenly crumpled to the ground sobbing, her arms hugging her body, rocking back and forth, the gun dangling from her fingers.

Gilly ran up the stairs to her side, took the gun from her fingers still squeezing the grip, handing it to Gramps as she wrapped her arms around Helen, holding her tight. Helen continued rocking in Gilly's tight embrace.

Skip turned the corner into the driveway. Gramps held up the gun the silver metal barrel sparkling in the sunlight. He signaled to Skip to come, to look down at the ground in front of the cars. As Skip rounded his Jeep he heard then saw the gray-haired woman sobbing in Gilly's arms. Heard Gilly trying to comfort her, telling her over and over again that she was going to be okay. He then saw Robyn lying on her back, holding a white bunny, thumb in her mouth, eyes wide open in the shade of the umbrella.

Skip helped Gilly and the sobbing grandmother to their feet. They walked her to Gilly's car and into the back seat. Gramps climbed in beside her, put his arm around her and held her hand. Helen's head fell to Gramps shoulder. The sobs subsided but the tears continued to stream down her face. Her breathing labored.

Gilly sat Robyn in her car seat as Skip located the car keys in Helen's car hanging from the ignition where she had left them. With a couple of nods between Skip and Gilly, they agreed that Skip would drive Helen's car. Skip put the gun on the seat beside him, pulled out of the driveway, let Gilly pass and followed her. She and Gramps were taking the distraught woman home to her husband.

Mr. Churchill, tears in his eyes as he spoke with his son in New York and what his plans were to claim his grandson's body from the prison morgue, was unaware of his wife's disappearance from the house. He was startled, dropping the phone, when Gilly pushed open the front door and saw Clay Wilder holding his wife as she staggered into the house.

Mr. Churchill took over holding his wife and guided her into the bedroom. With Gramps help they managed to get her on the bed. Gilly rushed in with a glass of water, held Helen's head up and urged her to take a few sips. Helen would have none of it slapping the glass out of Gilly's hand then rolled over, pulling a pillow into her body and continued to sob.

"She'll be okay in a little while," Mr. Churchill said. "It's just that it is such a shock …about Edward … the way he died. Thank you for bringing her home. I'll take care of her."

He shuffled out of the bedroom, Gilly and Gramps following, Gramps hand resting on Gilly's shoulder as they entered the living room.

Skip was sitting next to Robyn in her car seat when the three came into the room. Mr. Churchill put the dangling phone receiver to his ear then hung up the phone. Skip stood up and handed the gun to Mr. Churchill. "You might want to put this in a safe place, a place your wife doesn't know about."

Mr. Churchill looked at Skip. His face blank, uncomprehending. He looked at Gramps. "Was there trouble?"

"Nothing we can't deal with, but Skip's right. Maybe just get rid of it."

They said goodbye, Gilly adding that if Mr. Churchill needed any help to please call.

Skip slid in behind the wheel of Gilly's car as she and Gramps climbed in the back seat next to Robyn for the trip back to Hansville. No one spoke. Gilly and Gramps had literally dodged a couple of bullets.

Chapter 24

Skip swept Gilly's car down the driveway and pulled in behind his Jeep. The car came to a stop. Gilly, Gramps and Skip sat ... waiting. Waiting for what? Someone to come along and wipe the images from their mind of what had happened an hour ago?

Robyn's lower lip quivered followed by a wail. It was passed time for her bottle and nap.

Her cry was a call to action and everyone climbed out of the car, trooped down to the house with Robyn in her mother's arms. Gilly warmed a bottle and settled Robyn in her crib. Strong sucking emptied half the milk and then she fell asleep, the bottle falling to her side.

Gilly quietly pulled the guest bedroom door shut and joined Gramps and Skip in the kitchen. Gramps nodded at the steaming cup of tea waiting for her on the kitchen table. She sat down, took a sip, the heat soothing as the tea slid down her throat.

"Gramps, do we have to report what just happened?" Gilly asked in a soft voice, breaking the silence with the question the men had been pondering.

"I don't think so," Gramps replied continuing to stare out the window at the water. Clouds had moved in and the sparkling water had turned to a dull gray. "What do you say, Skip?"

"You've got a window with a hole in it and bad cracks. It has to be replaced. You're bound to be asked by a window guy what happened. In normal conversation, the question would be asked not really caring about the answer—passing the time of day as he replaces the window.

You could say anything—you accidentally hit it with a hammer fixing the gutter on the roof."

"Trouble is, we don't know what Helen's state of mind will be after she calms down," Gilly said. "Mr. Churchill will probably call her doctor … ask for a prescription for sleeping pills. Seems like we should tell someone in case she's totally snapped."

"You're right," Gramps said. "I'll call Detective Kracker over in Bremerton. No so much asking him to do something, but just to get the incident on the record."

"Good. Now, I have to get going," Gilly said taking her cup to the sink.

"How about a walk on the beach? Settle the nerves before you leave?" Skip asked.

"Okay. Nice change of subject. You can tell me how your run went this morning."

"And, missy, I've started a new exposé … more of a novel. People and places are changed to protect the innocent," he said laughing.

"Intriguing." Gilly smiled at him. "Robyn's still sleeping. We won't be gone long, Gramps."

Even though clouds covered the sun it was still over ninety. A slight breeze off the water tempered the oppressive humidity somewhat. The tide was out leaving packed sand mixed with small stones and cracked empty clam shells. They still had to navigate around the slimy green kelp with the odor of the vegetation baking in the sun.

"So, mystery man, what's this new exposé about?"

"You'll recognize the storyline—a double blackmail."

Gilly stopped walking and glowered at Skip. He didn't realize she had stopped, his head down, hands jammed into the pockets of his running shorts. He turned to see why she wasn't beside him. Grinning, he asked her, "What's the matter?"

"Oh, not much. Maybe a lot. This double blackmail wouldn't have anything to do with a pregnant girl and a married man would it?"

She said the words in an even tone but her arms were locked over her chest, and eyes sharpened. He saw trouble brewing.

"Kinda. But the story starts long before the girl and the man met, a foreigner who was hell bent on seducing the young woman. It starts with a New Yorker stealing her designs, and follows with his vendetta against the girl, sending her red satin hearts with a steel spike through—"

"Stop right there."

Trouble had boiled over and was about to hit him in the face.

"Hey, I told you names, places—

Gilly cut him off.

"Yeah ... names, places, etcetera, etcetera, etcetera will be changed to protect the innocent, I believe was the way you put it. Bullshit! How dare you tell my story for the world to read, ponder, dissect. A very painful, very very painful time in my life, a time I'm still trying to work through."

"I didn't mean to hurt you," Skip said holding his palms up to ward off her words.

"Hurt me? You bet it hurts ... me, my family, my baby girl when she grows up. It's my story to tell if I choose. Not yours." Gilly turned on her heel, sneakers slapping down on the sharp stones, marching back to the ladder and rickety stairs.

Skip ran after her. "Come on, Gilly. The bad part is behind you. You've moved on. You have a business—which, by the way, in case you haven't noticed, takes *all* of your time."

She whirled around, hands on her hips, her green eyes sending daggers in his direction. "How do you know what's behind me and what's in front of me? And, I'll do what I want, what I have to do with my time. That's what your doing isn't it? What you want—running a marathon, writing exposés, exposés of your friends' personal lives!

"Well, maybe we both need a little balance in our lives. There's more to life than work, you know. You're a pigheaded redhead. Maybe someday you'll figure out what's important."

"Believe me, I'm working on it." She took the ladder then the stairs in a blast of furry, ran into the house, gathered her things, and then put Robyn in the car.

Gramps hustled out the patio door, "Hey, sweetie, are you leaving?"

She hurried back to him, gave him a bear hug, and kissed him on the cheek. "I'll call to let you know I'm back safely at the shop. Let me know how it goes with the window and what Detective Kracker says." She pasted a smile on her face and left.

Darting out of the driveway, turning south on Hansville road, she kept her foot down on the gas pedal, slapping the steering wheel. The ferry was still loading cars as she pulled into line, bumping over the ramp. The crewman signaled for her to start a new row and she curved to go down the outside lane to the front of the vessel. Turning the key in the ignition the engine stopped. Gilly leaned back in the seat exhaling a blast of air. The fight was gone. Her breathing back to normal.

Checking Robyn in the rearview mirror, she saw her baby had fallen asleep.

Gilly opened the windows to feel the breeze off the water from the ferry churning its way to Seattle. First in line on the ferry was like being on a balcony of a cruise ship—the panorama of the water, the nearby islands looked close enough that you could almost reach out to the beaches and trees. What an awful day, she thought.

What in the world was Skip thinking—double blackmail? Dragging her personal life out into the open. Open? She hadn't even come to grips with her life. It was sweeping her along—day to day, week to week, month to month. "I wonder if he asked Philip if he minded his story showing up in print?" she said talking to Robyn in the mirror. "I wonder if he let Philip read the manuscript or was I the only one? It didn't bother me when I read about Eleanor being a money grubber. It wasn't my story. But to read that a stupid girl went to Paris and got pregnant, that would be awful. Same thing. Except … one is about me. Maybe Philip doesn't know what's in Skip's *exposé*. *Exposé* —good word. My bad choices exposed."

He called me pigheaded, she thought. I wonder if any of my other friends think I'm pigheaded? Nicole? Gabby? Oh, I hope Maria doesn't think I'm pigheaded. Have I been too assertive? Starting my business has been hard. I have to make decisions. They want me to make the hard choices, don't they?

Sounds like Edward had a horrible death. I'll have to call DuBois. Find out. Helen blamed me and Gramps. His death wasn't our fault. I refuse to take that one on. Edward did steal my designs; he had his hands on my throat. Gramps is a good shot, he could have killed Edward that day but instead he shot him in the foot to stop him. Edward made bad choices, but I feel sorry for Helen. She's been so good to me over the years. Supportive. She didn't mean what she did today.

What was it Skip said—"a Frenchman hell bent on seducing the girl?" Maxime did take advantage of me but there was more to it. That's the problem with putting things in print—black and white. Life is not black and white. Take what I said to Skip in the hospital … I love you. Thank God he was asleep. What was I really saying? Love as in loving a friend? I was still drugged, just had a baby, alone. Did I mean love for a friend, or love as in lover?

A horn let out a blast signaling their arrival at Pier 52. The ferry bumped against the pilings, the engines grinding in reverse, as it came to a stop.

Gilly turned the key in the car's ignition and waited for the crew to drop the chains so she could drive off. "I know, I'll to talk to Gramps." She smiled thinking about her grandfather. He was a good listener, but more important, without saying anything, he had a way of setting her straight.

Chapter 25

The door into the design studio burst open. Nicole scooted in and closed the door, leaned back against it, breathing hard from running up the stairs. Her eyes were wide as if she had just seen a ghost.

"Gilly, you have a visitor."

"Nicole, please ask Gabby to find out what she wants. I'm about to leave for Hansville."

"It's not a her. It's a him."

"Who is it?" Gilly asked puzzled. Now, who has Nicole so worked up, she wondered.

"Maxime. Maxime Beaumont is downstairs. He just waltzed in. Asked for you. I can't believe it. What do you want me to tell him?"

Gilly's wide-eyed stare matched Nicole's. He was certainly the last person she expected to walk into her shop. Had she missed a letter? A telephone message? He couldn't be wondering if she had received the baby clothes. She had sent him a note immediately thanking him for Robyn's gifts. That was all she said—*thanks* and signed her name. Maybe he was miffed she didn't say more, go on and on how kind he was. No, he couldn't have expected that.

"Well, tell him I was about to leave but I can spare a minute. Bring him to the studio. And, Nicole, leave the door open."

"Yeah. Okay." Nicole turned, leaving with the clicking of her heels in her wake as she navigated the stairs.

Gilly felt her chest tighten. She reached to turn off her tablet, drew back her hand. It was shaking. This is ridiculous, she thought. Calm down. Breathe deep.

She felt his presence before he spoke. She slowly raised her eyes. He was standing in the doorway looking around the new studio, then his eyes moved to her, taking her in. "Every time I see you, you are more beautiful. But you are working too hard. I can see it in your eyes."

"I didn't know you were coming. I was about to leave for—"

"Would you have seen me if I told you I was coming?"

"Probably not."

"Ah, see." He shook his head and smiled. "Where are you going that you have to leave this minute."

"To Gramp's. I left some things there last weekend. Mom and Dad are coming over for a quick lunch so they can see Robyn, and—"

"Ah, a family visit. How wonderful. I will come with you that way I can spend some time with our little girl."

"Oh, no." Gilly shook her head. "No, that would not be a good idea. My dad—"

"Your dad will what? Punch me? I wouldn't blame him."

"He might," Gilly flashed a quick smile.

"There. There's a smile. Where's Robyn?"

Gilly looked toward the door into her apartment. "Maria's changing her, she—"

The door opened and Maria stepped through holding Robyn. "Oh, I'm sorry, I didn't mean to interrupt."

"You didn't. Maria, this is Maxime Beaumont. Maxime, this is Maria Jackson, my friend."

Maria was dumbfounded. Her jaw dropped as Maxime strode over to her, carefully lifting Robyn from her arms.

"No, I—"

"It's okay, Maria. Maxime seems to think he wants to meet my parents and Gramps. I told him it might not be pleasant but he wants to anyway. We should be back before dark."

The trip to Hansville was strained at first, then Gilly began to relax. A little. In the car Maxime turned in his seat so he could study her and gaze at Robyn strapped in her carrier in the back seat. They didn't say much, but he made an occasional remark—enjoying the ferry cruise, the waters of Puget Sound, the Seattle skyline as it receded from view. But, he said many times how delightful Robyn was—so petite, her tiny hands, and red curls.

He was captivated by the towering pines lining Hansville Road, the occasional fields of produce, and the roadside stands where the lettuce, corn and tomatoes were sold as well as strawberries. Lots of strawberries.

Gilly stole a glance at him, smiled, quickly looked away. She had alerted her grandfather to the passenger she was bringing. He said he'd pass along the alert to her mom and dad—they were arriving any minute.

Gilly didn't know what to expect when Maxime showed up at the house. As far as they were concerned Gilly had not had any communication with him since the day she walked out on him at the restaurant in Paris when he told her he and his wife were reconciling. She hadn't told them of his previous visit, or the presents he had sent to their baby. *Their* baby? When did she start thinking of her baby as *theirs*? She shook her head.

"What's the matter, Gillianne? Are you worried about your parents? I promise you I will be a gentleman no matter what they say. Let me be sure of their names. Your mother is Anne, father's Will, and your grandfather's Clay."

"That's right. And yes, of course, I'm worried. This is crazy, Maxime. I should drop you off at that gas station. Pick you up on my way back."

"But you won't. You are a strong woman, and I bet you are a little intrigued about how this meeting will unfold."

Again she shook her head, but this time with a small sly smile. He had her pegged. Well, whatever was going to transpire she would know in a few minutes. She turned down the long driveway and parked next to her parent's car.

Maxime got out, opened her car door, then opened the back door. Releasing the seatbelt buckle he lifted the sleeping infant in her carrier out of the car. "May I carry her?"

Gilly nodded, yes. She wasn't sure her legs were going to hold her up.

Gramps was the first out the patio door, then her mother who put her arm thru her father-in-laws for support, and then her father emerged, hands on his hips. Gramps had a smile on his face. Gilly thought if someone dropped in out of the sky they would see a happy couple bringing their baby to visit her happy grandparents. Wrong! Nothing could have been further from the truth.

Given the looks on their faces, Gilly introduced Maxime to her mother and grandfather first relieving Maxime of the carrier. Gramps immediately stuck out his hand and the two men greeted each other with a strong grip.

Her mother gave a nod in his direction as she whispered, "Maxime." Maxime in turn bowed his head to her, "Anne, it's a pleasure to meet you."

Then it was her father's turn. "My father, Will. Maxime."

Maxime smiled with a slight nod. "Nice to meet you, Will."

Her father stood his ground. Hostility written on his face. No smile.

"Well, now that the pleasantries are over, how about a bite of lunch?" Gramps said. "Come on Maxime, you haven't tasted anything with eggs until you've tried one of Anne's quiches."

Good old Gramps, Gilly thought. Always to my rescue.

Maxime stood to the side as everyone passed through the door, down the hall and gathered around the kitchen table. As with anyone who first gazed out the kitchen's big picture window overlooking the sound, Maxime was no different. The warm weather and the sunshine provided an idyllic scene as a sailboat race passed by, their colorful spinnakers filled with wind pushing the small crafts through the sparkling blue water. On the far side, a tanker, high in the water, was skimming through the waves into Seattle to pick up cargo.

Nerves didn't relax much but enough so conversation wasn't too uncomfortable. However, it didn't take long to finish off Anne's quiche. Gilly excused herself to gather the items she had left and to feed Robyn, changing her for the trip back to Seattle.

Gramps stood up, pushed his chair back. "Maxime, how about a little tour of the garden?"

"Delighted to, Monsieur," Maxime said easily with a smile.

"Ah ha. Monsieur … I like that." With a twinkle in his eye, Gramps led the way to his den and the pictures above the wall-to-wall bookcases. He explained the various operations depicted at the Pope and Talbot lumber mill in Port Gamble where he had worked until they closed. "The lumber business stalled and they let go all the workers. Those were bad times around here. Fortunately my wife and I, Betty, Gilly's grandmother, had bought this place for our retirement and that's exactly what I did. Retired."

"Your work must have been physically demanding. Did Will work in the mill with you?"

"Yes, and he's had a hard time of it. However, he is an excellent carpenter and electrician. If there's work to be had, he's the first to be called. He's that good. Helped Gilly with the shop. Have you seen the shop?"

"Yes. Very sophisticated, yet warm, inviting … like your granddaughter." Maxime looked into Gramps blue eyes. Nothing to fear there. A wonderful man trying to support his granddaughter, treading carefully in the wake of a stranger's sudden appearance.

"Come on, son, let's go outside." They ambled up the strip of lawn in the backyard, picked a few raspberries. Maxime followed Gramp's lead and popped a juicy berry into his mouth. Gramps looked up, head turning sharply to his left. The road was on the other side of the dense thicket of blackberries. His eyes darted around the thicket, but nothing seemed amiss. He looked again, squinted, shrugged, and turned back to his guest, shoulders relaxing. Must have been his imagination.

"The view down over the bank is something you have to see." They strolled down the stretch of lawn, around the house, to the front and the rickety stairs. "Down there is a deck. Before the stairs became wiggly, we'd have Bloody Marys down there with our Sunday breakfast. The Queen Betty we called her. Afraid it's a bit in disrepair now. But at the time, Gilly would climb down the ladder and run into the surf of the incoming tide squealing at the top of her lungs, the waves freezing her toes."

Maxime turned to Gramps. "Clay, I have hurt your granddaughter, I know that. I was a stupid man with the love of my life within reach. I want you to know I'm not here to hurt her, never again. I want to be part of our baby's life … if she will let me."

"I'm glad to hear that, son. She's an exceptional young woman. Faced up to her pregnancy, a situation that no girl wants to find herself in. There was never the slightest thought of aborting, nor of parting with the child in an adoption. I don't know if there's a future for the two of you—she's never indicated that was in cards. On the contrary, I'm surprised she let you in the door." Gramps chuckled.

"What about her father. Is he going to give her a hard time for bringing me out to meet the family?"

"Not a hard time. But, it may take him awhile to understand why she brought you to us. Maybe none of us understands."

"But you, Clay, you understand." Maxime said looking again deep into Gramp's faded blue eyes.

"Yes, I understand. I'm glad you came to Seattle. It was the right thing to do, and it is the right thing to do everything you can to be part of that sweet baby's life. I thank you for having the decency, the courage, and I dare say the love to face her."

"Thank you, Clay. I'm glad I came too. And, you're right. I love your granddaughter, fell in love with her the first time I saw her modeling in Paris. I've trampled on that love, but I'll keep the love for our baby close to my heart."

Chapter 26

Week five—eleven to go. Skip checked his shoes. They were showing wear but okay for another couple of weeks. Nonetheless he had packed a new pair in his gym. He was psyched for today's long run. He wondered if Gilly would show up at Gramp's today. She hadn't come to cheer him on last weekend. He didn't ask, and Gramps didn't volunteer a reason why she didn't show.

By the time Skip had stretched in the driveway, slipped four Gatorades in his backpack, Agatha was sound asleep in the doorway to the kitchen, a paw resting on top of her rawhide bone. Coco was curled up next to her. They were friends again.

Starting at a slow trot, Skip felt strong, mentally preparing for the ten-mile run. Rounding a curve in the road he saw Gilly's car approaching. She slowed, waved, and continued on down the road.

A smile on his face, Skip had to restrain himself not to pick up his pace. But, he knew that was a no-no. He must stay in his zone or risk injury.

He relaxed his neck and shoulders, filled his mind with positive images of his feet striking the pavement in an even cadence, and focused on his breathing.

In. In.
Out. Out.
In. In.
Out. Out.

A car traveling in the opposite direction gave him a wide birth. It was immediately followed by the same motorcycle he had seen several times before—a man driving with the woman behind. They didn't wave and were going north for the first time since he had started running on Hansville Road.

He'd had a good training week. Including the ten miles today, he will have run twenty-one miles breaking the twenty-mile barrier. He figured he'd be out on the road for almost two hours, at his slow training pace and had to watch his fluid intake. He switched to all Gatorade for this long run to replace energy and electrolytes in addition to the fluid. He knew that the added carbs helped maintain his energy near the end of the race when he was apt to hit the wall. Oh he remembered that wall but he had managed to break through it in Oklahoma.

He drank two cups of water on the ferry to hydrate his body before he started his long run today. Mandatory. Water consumption was important within two hours before he ran, during a run, and for three hours following his run.

He was schooled to look at his urine on non-running days. If it was pale, he was keeping himself hydrated. No coffee or alcohol was permitted that would flush precious liquid from his body before, during, or immediately after a run. It was the first week of September and the heat had broken. It should be even cooler on race day, he thought.

Skip reached around and pulled a bottle from his backpack, downed about eight ounces, capped it, returned it to the pack. He drank the same amount on the order of every two miles. He had driven his route, five miles out and return, noting landmarks that he would pass approximately every two miles.

Today he was working on his mental toughness. His coach had drilled into his runners the power of visualization. "Make two short mental tapes—each one to two minutes long," he said. The first was to be about the best run he ever had. Where he ran, what he saw, smelled. What he wore, what was the weather like, and how he felt. He remembered the crowds along the way cheering and imagined they were cheering for him. Why not? It was his video.

In. In.

Out. Out.

The second tape was at the finish of the marathon. He was to imagine what he looked like, who will be there, what he will say to them, what they will say to him. He had written notes about his mental videos in college, dug them out during the week and put them to memory again. He started the first tape. He was in Oklahoma, hot, his clothing was light, he felt great. Why not? I won that race. He smiled and played the tape in his mind again.

Who was there? He played over tape two—his coach, his fellow runners. After catching his breath he congratulated the others, but they treated him like a hero. "Hunter, you won. Hunter, you won," they chanted. It was wonderful. He edited the tape. Gilly was there, smiling, cheering. He played the tape again.

Running down the driveway, Skip waved to Gilly standing next to the playpen. Robyn watched him perform his cool-down stretching routine.

He and Gilly hadn't spoken since their quarrel and he had his apology framed in his mind. He had been an idiot, not that she was blameless, but what had possessed him to say she was a pigheaded redhead … well, he was mad.

"How was the run? How far?" Gilly asked as he ambled down the steps.

"Ten miles, and it felt great. Gilly, I—"

She stopped him, waving her palm at him. "It's okay."

"No, it's not okay. I'm sorry. I was wrong. It was a stupid argument—"

"You weren't entirely wrong," she said with a grin. "I am a redhead, can be stubborn. Maybe that falls under the category of pigheaded."

He stood awkwardly, shifting from one foot to the other, hands jammed in the pockets of his running shorts.

"I'm sorry, Skip. Truce?"

"Truce. If I wasn't so sweaty I'd seal it with a hug but—"

"Skip, look up at the berry patch."

He followed her gaze, scanned the area about thirty-five yards away, turned back. "What did you see?"

"I don't know … somebody moving in the bushes maybe." Squinting, hands shielding her eyes, she continued to scan the back yard, her eyes darting from one side to the other. Letting her arms drop she said, "Imagining things I guess. Come on in, Gramps has lunch ready for you. Fish again," she said with a grin. "Maybe you can talk him into buying some chicken breasts next week."

Skip held the patio door for her as she lifted Robyn from the playpen and walked into the house.

Finishing up the last of the baked salmon, the doorbell rang.

"Finish your lunch, you two. I'll see who that is. About time for the mail. Maybe I have a package. Ordered some special socks for our marathoner," Gramps said grinning. He returned a few minutes later, shrugged, and proceeded to pour boiling water from the kettle over the teabags, decaf, into the three mugs.

"Who was that, Gramps." Gilly asked clearing the table.

"Some guy. Lawn maintenance. Wanted to know if I'd like him to spread fertilizer before winter. Something about the rain would soak it in. Make it lush. That's all I need—a lush lawn requiring more mowing." He shook his head and set the steamy mugs on the table.

Chapter 27

What to do?

Wellington wanted major changes to his story.

The returned manuscript was in his mailbox when he got home from work. Skip reread Philip's notes.

Wellington okayed the first chapter on his background—his struggles trying to make a go of his cattle ranch in Montana. But it was downhill from there on. He thought he came off too surly with his staff; thought Eleanor sounded too supportive and wasn't as beautiful as Skip said; too much credit to the reporter in the story and the tipsters who had called him and not enough to the detective, DuBois, and the police work. He also demanded he add that most people felt Eleanor should receive the death penalty and not life in prison for the murder of Gerald Sacco. "I don't care if a body was never found," Philip wrote.

Skip stared at the shredder beside his computer table.

He strolled into the kitchen. Looked at the refrigerator. A six-pack was in there. He wanted to drink them all.

Something dropped on his foot. Agatha's leash. She let out a soft whine.

"You're right, Aggie. Better to go for a run. He picked up her leash, checked his training schedule for the beginning of week six: Tuesday, four miles. He looked at Aggie again. "Do you think you can run for a mile, girl?"

Skip snapped on her leash. "I don't want any side trips checking out that poodle, or the squirrels. A pee and a poop is all you get then I bring you home and I finish the run."

They headed out of the condo building and across the street to the park. Agatha was thrilled to be out and broke the rules immediately doing a roundy-round with a beagle. After fifteen minutes of sniffing, peeing, and pooping, Agatha settled down to a brisk walk beside her master. However, Skip couldn't focus.

His plan had been to give Wellington selected chapters for his comment. But after Gilly's reaction to his idea of writing her story, he thought he'd better send Wellington the entire manuscript on the gold heist. Now he was sorry. He hated rewrites. The shredder and the delete key on his computer keyboard looked good.

"Don't be such a baby, Hunter."

He felt a tug on the leash. Agatha wanted to change direction.

He followed his dog. Heck, it didn't matter where he ran. Just keep going, he thought.

His idea of writing exposés suddenly turned sour. People were going to have issues with the way they were portrayed. Shit, he was the writer. He could write it the way he wanted. Couldn't he?

The image of Gilly's explosion filled his head. He was startled by her reaction to his writing a story about a double blackmail. Of course, she had a point. It was going to be about her. Everything was about her. He wanted her. She was a package deal—she and Robyn. He was okay with that. Besides, they could have their own baby someday. But there was that wide moat around her. The barrier seemed to be shrinking until he talked about the double blackmail. "Stick to your plan, Hunter. Run the marathon, get your head on straight. The way forward will be clear. It'll all work out especially if she continues to come out to Gramps on the weekends—nine more and then the race.

Agatha stopped. Sat down. Skip pulled on her leash but she wouldn't budge so Skip sat next to her on the grass.

I probably should check again with DuBois, he thought. Go over the facts about Eleanor Wellington, and get the final report on Edward Churchill's violent death.

He gave his hound's silky head a pat and a gentle scratch behind her ears. "What should I do about smoothing things over with Gilly, Agatha?"

Aggie got up, shook her rotund body, and slurped a kiss on Skip's cheek.

"You're right. It's high time I gave her a good kiss. Come on, girl, let's go home. I have work to do."

"Hey, Skipper."

He recognized her voice.

Diane ran up to him, gave Aggie a pat.

"I wondered if I might run into you. No pun intended," she said smiling. "How about grabbing something at the deli? Come back here. There's a picnic table over there."

"Sorry, Di. Just giving Aggie a quick walk. Some other time. See you at the newsroom tomorrow."

Diane watched as Skip jogged off in the direction of his condo, Agatha by his side.

Chapter 28

Maxime's visit seemed to fade into the distant past. When the girls asked Gilly about it, she simply shrugged and said the meeting with her parents had gone relatively well, all things considered. It was as if he had crossed the ocean, and a continent, landing in Seattle and then immediately lifted off for a return flight to Paris.

It was Saturday morning and Gilly was rushing around preparing for her weekly trip to Hansville to visit with Gramps and to cheer Skip on, have lunch and return. Pulling Robyn's arms through the sleeves of the sweater, she shouted out to Gabby to call her at Gramps if the customer who dropped into the shop yesterday afternoon came back ready to order. The lady, a prominent Seattle attorney, had been very excited over finding the collection and had tried on numerous combinations. She purchased a suit-dress and indicated she would be back soon. She said she was going straight home to clean out her closet. There was a good possibility that a large order would come of her visit.

Gabby stood in the doorway of Gilly's bedroom as she stuffed her E-tablet and a pair of shorts in her bag. Without looking up, Gilly said, "I doubt I'll need these shorts but if the sun comes out maybe Robyn and I can spend a few minutes outside."

"How far is Skip running today? Gabby asked.

"Twelve miles." She looked at Gabby with a grimace on her face. "Can you believe it? I huff and puff running up and down the stairs a few times a day."

Swinging the bag over her shoulder, she scooped up Robyn into the other arm and left with a wave in Gabby's direction.

Spotting Skip ahead nearing a vegetable stand, she slowed down and waved. He waved back, giving her a thumbs up as she passed. He looks good, she thought. Very focused. Those blue eyes of his intense as always.

"What do you think, Robyn?" she asked glancing in the rearview mirror at her daughter, reaching back to give her chubby leg a squeeze. "Are you going to run a marathon some day?"

Robyn watched at her mother, her pink lips puckering under her big dark eyes.

Concentrating on the road, Gilly reached back again giving a little tug on Robyn's foot. "Mommy loves you, baby girl."

Checking her watch, she smiled as she parked behind Skip's Jeep. She had bettered her usual two-hour travel time by fifteen minutes. A sunny day and I see Gramps has already put the playpen out on the lawn, she thought. Entering the patio door, she gave Agatha a pat on the head, and continued down the hall to tell Gramps she had arrived.

There was a note on the kitchen table that he and Anne had run into Poulsbo for some serious marathon food and would be back about one o'clock. Also, that he thought she might like to sit outside so the playpen and lounger were ready.

It was eleven-thirty and the sun was wonderful—bright and warm. "All right, baby girl, you and mommy are going to sit in the sun. This is something girls do—sunbathe." Smiling, she kissed Robyn's chubby cheek and walked outside. Gilly positioned the umbrella on the playpen to shield Robyn from the direct rays of the sun and then settled into the lounger and closed her eyes, relishing the warmth of the sun on her skin. Robyn jabbered then, tucking the white bunny under her arm, put her thumb in her mouth. A couple of sucks and her hand fell to her side.

Hearing the phone, Gilly darted in the patio door to answer it. Gabby immediately shrieked that the woman from yesterday did indeed come in and ordered over $2000 worth of clothes—almost everything from the entire fall line, and two of some in different fabrics. Because a few of the items weren't in stock, Gabby told her she would able to fill her order before the end of next week.

"Maybe I should leave more often," Gilly laughed. "Good job, Gab. See you tonight."

"Well, as Maria would say, you got that right girlfriend."

Smiling, Gilly returned to the lounger, put her hand over her eyes blocking the sun and gazed over at Robyn.

The playpen was empty!

Chapter 29

*G*ramps!

"Mom!

"Skip!"

Gilly screamed running up the steps to the driveway. Her car was there. Skip's car was there.

She was alone.

Her baby was gone.

She raced down the steps, slammed through the patio door tripping on the sill she fell to the cement, her hands scrapping the floors rough surface. Scrambling to her feet she raced to the kitchen, lifted the receiver. Her trembling fingers dropped it. Snatching the receiver off the floor with one hand she jabbed 911 with the other.

"911 Operator. What's your emergency?"

"My baby's gone," Gilly screamed into the phone. "Someone's taken her. Help me."

"Your name?"

"Gillianne Wilder, Hansville. Please, help me."

"How long has your baby been missing?"

"About ... about ... about twenty minutes."

"Are you sure the toddler didn't crawl—

"She's only six-and-a-half months old. She was in the playpen outside. I answered the phone. She's gone!"

"Your address?"

Gilly gave the woman Gramp's address and slammed the phone down. Running outside she looked at the playpen again. She has to be there, she thought. Her breathing erratic, heart racing, she looked at her watch. Skip wouldn't be back for another forty-five minutes at best, forty or more for her mom. She dashed back in the house, fumbled in her tote for her cell.

"Mom—

"Oh, Gilly. We just bought the most beautiful cod—

"Mom, Robyn's gone. Mom, someone took her." Gilly struggled to retain her composure but tears began streaming down her face. Terrified, she gulped for air. Walked back outside. Looked in the playpen.

"Did you call 911," Anne asked, the car accelerating with the pressure of her foot on the gas pedal.

"Yes. Yes. But, Mom, they're thirty minutes away."

"Your grandfather and I will be there in about twenty minutes. Call your father. Has Skip returned?"

"No."

"Call him. I'm sure he has his cell phone with him."

A gray sedan bumped over the ramp onto the Kingston to Edmond's ferry. It was the last car to load. The ramp immediately lifted into place as the ferry pulled away from the pilings. The man behind the wheel and the woman in the backseat holding a baby girl laid their heads back, each expelling air with a whoosh.

"Do you think that man we passed will remember the car?" the woman asked as she tried to soothe the baby who had begun to whimper.

"Might. We've seen him every Saturday for the past seven weeks. I'm going to get a cup of coffee. Want one? I don't think you should go up on deck."

"Yes. What is it, thirty minutes to Edmonds?"

"Thirty-four if you believe the printed schedule. We lucked out all around. Baby left alone, perfect timing to get this ferry. I didn't want to go the Bainbridge—too far. We would have run a big risk of a roadblock."

"How's the timing for the plane?"

"Well, with lighter traffic than a weekday, we should be able to get to the airport in just under an hour, then park, clear security, and board. No bags. You're sure you have the passports?"

"Yes. Stop asking."

"Hey, don't get snarly with me. I paid a lot for that kid's passport. The cell phone picture the woman gave me worked like a charm. The hardest part is done. Now it's just a matter of the damn plane taking off on time, our connections being on time, and then we handoff the kid to the woman and she hands us a hundred Gs. Not bad pay for twenty-four hours of fear and tension," the man said as he chuckled. "Just don't let that kid cry. You know how I get—crazy. Sit tight. I'll be back in a jiff with your coffee."

"Get one of those little cartons of milk if they have it, if not then a water. I'll slip a little of the sedative stuff in her bottle. And, for God's sake, keep that damn temper of yours under control, or I swear I'll—

"Shut your fat mouth and be careful. That doctor said he didn't approve of giving a baby anything to sleep, especially when you told him *your friend's* baby was under a year. We're lucky he gave it to us."

"Don't you tell me to shut up. You shut up. Go get the milk. I wish we'd never agreed to this."

"Yeah? Well, you'll be happy enough when you have the money to throw around in Paris," the man said, slamming the car door.

The woman lifted the baby to her shoulder patting its back. The baby whimpered, her face turning red. She was about to howl bloody murder.

Chapter 30

Gilly strode into the kitchen, leaned on the dryer—hands splayed on the edge, head down, lips pursed tight into a thin line.

"Be strong. Be strong," she said over and over. "I'll find you, Robyn. Mommy is going to find you."

Hearing a car roll into the driveway, she raced out the patio door. Three doors flew open—Anne, Gramps, and Skip emerged. They had picked up Skip down the road. He was the first to reach her, gave her a fierce hug, then pushed her away at arm's length, holding her by the shoulders, his intense blue eyes searching her face.

"What's the latest?" he asked.

"The police should be here in a few minutes."

"How long has it been?"

"Less than an hour."

"And?"

"That's it." Gilly responded staring back.

Anne squeezed in front of Skip and hugged her daughter, and then Gramps was by her side. "Come on child, let's go sit down. Tell us exactly what happened."

Each looked away from the empty playpen as they passed into the house.

Anne put the kettle on the stove. Skip sat at one end of the table, Gramps the other next to Gilly. He placed his veined, leathery hand over hers, the pair looking into each other's eyes for comfort.

Gilly shot to her feet hearing a car park in the driveway. It was Deputy Kracker and his partner Claire Troxell. Escorting them into the kitchen they sat down to hear what Gilly had to say about the disappearance of her baby.

Troxell asked Gilly for a picture, several if she had them, of baby Robyn.

Kracker had contacted Detective DuBois in Seattle, explaining the situation. DuBois told him there would be an immediate Amber alert displayed on all western Washington's highways, and the media would flash the alert on their news broadcasts. Deputy Troxell emailed pictures of Robyn to the Bremerton office as well as to DuBois—within minutes Robyn's picture was dispatched to over a hundred squad cars, officers, and transportation points—ferry, bus, train, and airport.

The gray sedan bumped over the ramp and off the ferry at Edmonds. The man drove the speed limit through the small town, and then merged onto I-5 south to SeaTac airport. The clock was still favoring their getaway.

Ditching the car in the parking garage, the man dropped his cigarette on the cement, and the pair raced to the terminal—the woman clutching the drugged baby, the man running with three shoulder bags banging against his arms and back. Cleared through security showing passports with their tickets, they ran up to the check-in counter for seat assignments pushing three open tickets to Chicago in front of the female attendant—he was taking no chances on a hold up because of the baby. Luck was with them—the flight was not overbooked. Seat assignments in hand, they scampered down the jetway. They were the last to board the plane.

The stewardess helped to buckle them in their seats.

The plane slowly pulled away from the gate. The plane was cleared for takeoff. The plane gained speed over the tarmac and was quickly airborne.

DuBois called Gilly with an urgent request. "Reporters are asking to speak with you. I suggest you return to Seattle as soon as you can. Your personal appearance on television will bring more attention to your missing baby. You can help get the story out to the public faster if you're here and better for ongoing news reports. Have available the most recent pictures of the baby. The networks will get them on the air and send them to the local papers."

"All right. I'll leave immediately," Gilly replied.

"Call me just before you drive off the ferry. I'll tell you where to go, however, it may be best to go straight to your apartment. I can have an officer escort you to meet with the media. In any event, give me a call."

"Okay, Detective, and thank you."

"Put Deputy Kracker on the line, please. But, Gilly, you get on your way."

Gilly handed the phone to Deputy Kracker and then faced her family. "DuBois wants me back in Seattle. Said the networks can get the story out faster if I'm readily available."

"I'll drive you," Skip said. "Get your things. I'll be in the car."

"Thanks, but I'm going to want to have my car available, but I'd appreciate your following me." She kissed her mom and Gramps, grabbed her tote and rocketed out the door, pausing at the playpen for the white bunny. It was missing, too.

Kracker called to her to wait. "Gilly, I've put in a call for an officer and his search and rescue dog. He's bringing a couple of deputies. They'll start a search of the yard, the neighbors, the road. Maybe they can come up with some clues. I've also asked Skip to stay so we can interview him unless you really need him."

"No, that's okay."

Skip joined her, took the tote off her shoulder, and walked her to her car. "I told Kracker I've been running here every Saturday for seven weeks. There's a motorcycle, passed me on almost every run. Maybe I can help. I'll call you when I'm back in Seattle. And, please let me know if there are any changes."

"I will. Thanks." Skip gave her a brief hug, set the tote in her car and shut the door. The wheels spun out of the driveway, darting south onto Hansville Road and out of sight behind a stand of pine trees.

"Troxell, you wait here for the other deputies and the dog," Kracker said. "I guess the dog can pick up the baby's scent from that bonnet in the playpen. I'll ask Gilly's mother for a picture and anything else she might have that could be helpful. Hunter, come with me. Tell me about that motorcycle. Being a reporter you should be able to give me a pretty good description," Kracker said over his shoulder as he strode into the house.

Chapter 31

The story of baby Robyn Wilder's kidnapping flooded the evening news. Her mother, Gillianne Wilder of Gillianne Wilder Fashions was interviewed and pictures of the curly red-haired child were seen by millions.

The story quickly spread from the west coast to the east coast. Anyone watching was immediately taken with the plight of the young mother.

At 8:15 p.m. an American Airline's flight from Seattle landed at Chicago's O'Hare airport. The passengers disembarked, among them a family with a very sleepy baby bundled in a footed sleeper. They made their way to a ticket counter to purchase tickets for the next flight to Paris. The agent suggested Turkish Airlines. If they hurried they would have time to board a flight leaving in two hours. The man thanked the attendant and asked how to get to the Turkish Airline terminal.

With the information, the man flagged down a transporter to drive them to Terminal 5, International Flights. As the couple with the baby were driven from American Airlines, they caught a brief CNN news report about a missing baby in Hansville, Washington. The baby's picture filled the screen for a few seconds with a tip line if anyone had information on the whereabouts of the infant. The woman rearranged the baby's blanket so a large piece of fabric covered the sleeping infant's head.

The transporter let the family off at the ticket counter for Turkish Airline. Now at Terminal 5 they did not see the news report air again. The woman poked the man and pointed to a newsstand displaying billed caps. The man nodded, hurried over to the display and purchased the smallest cap they had—blue with a Velcro adjuster tab in the back.

The man purchased tickets for the Turkish Airline 10:20 p.m. flight to Istanbul and the connection to Paris. The flight was scheduled to land at Ataturk International Airport at 5:05 p.m. the next day with a connecting flight departing Istanbul at 7:50 p.m. arriving Paris, Charles de Gaulle Airport at 10:30 p.m.

They immediately entered the line leading to the security attendant checking passports. The man handed the attendant their three passports and were told they could proceed to the gate. They walked to the gate and boarded the plane.

The plane took off on schedule. Destination: Turkey.

By morning of the next day the disappearance of the baby was capturing the hearts of Europeans over breakfast, stopping for coffee at a café, or reading the latest news on their electronic devices—cells, tablets, and computers.

Maxime flipped on his bedroom television as he knotted his tie. Pushing the knot in place under his collar he heard the reporter say the name Gillianne Wilder. Turning, he saw the picture of his baby holding the white bunny he had given her flash on the screen. The next frame displayed a reporter sitting next to Gillianne, stoically answering the reporter's questions, looking into the camera, asking for help in finding her child, her emerald eyes filled with pain.

The screen switched to a close-up of the reporter. "If anyone has information as to the whereabouts of this adorable baby girl, please call the tip line number on the bottom of your screen."

Maxime strode to his dresser, picked up Gillianne's business card, then picked up his bedside phone and punched in her number. Hearing her strangled voice on the other end his eyes closed.

"Gillianne … I just saw—

"Maxime?" she whispered.

"Yes, my darling. Have they found her?"

"No."

He could barely hear her. If only he could reach out and touch her, pull her tight, reassure her, support her, love …

"Maxime, what if …"

"No, no, you mustn't think the worst. Stay strong, my darling. You can … I know. What can I do to help … please … what can I do?"

"There's nothing … only wait … the police are trying very hard …"

Maxime left his apartment, hailed a cab, and asked to be taken to the Palais de Luxembourg, the seat of the French Parliament. The Senate was in session today. Maxime stopped briefly in his office and then joined the other senators and deputies in the meeting hall.

He couldn't concentrate on the legislation being discussed, his mind constantly wandering to Seattle and the welfare of the small infant, his baby, his and Gillianne's child. He allowed his head to drop, eyes to close, what in God's name would he do if anything happened to the baby he wondered?

The second he had seen her bright dark eyes, the clusters of red curls, he had fallen in love with her, the same as he had when he first laid eyes on her mother. When Robyn had grabbed his finger with her little fist he knew he would protect her with his life. So what was he doing here, this moment sitting in the seat of the French government, listening to speech after speech?

Excusing himself, he left the hall, left the building and strolled into the Luxembourg Garden, the largest and most beautiful park in Paris, a fifty-five acre public garden. Even though it was the end of September, the broad expanses of lawn remained a rich green, and the manicured flower beds where still ablaze with vibrant color.

Maxime stood still a moment, watching a mother with three toddlers speaking rapidly to her children. She turned to look at him and he saw she was holding an infant in her arms. She smiled, looked down at a little boy tugging at her skirt and continued walking.

Maxime wandered on and realized he had reached his apartment building. The sun was low in the sky, painting the Seine in ripples of gold. He crossed the street, slowly stepped down the old stairs to the benches beside the river. He sank onto a worn wooden bench supported by a black wrought-iron frame. Leaning forward, forearms on his legs, palms together, fingers forming a steeple, he asked God for his help, pleading with him to keep his baby safe, pleading that she be returned unharmed to her mother. Maxime did not think of himself as a religious man, but this hour he prayed, this hour he was a believer, this hour he needed and asked for God's help.

Returning to his apartment, he checked his phone for messages. There were none. It was 6:11 p.m.—9:11 a.m. in Seattle. He placed the call to Gillianne, listened to the rings, waiting for her to answer. The phone was picked up, but he didn't recognize the voice, a voice with a decided French accent.

"Mademoiselle, my name is Monsieur Beaumont."

"Oui, Monsieur, I'm Nicole."

"Ah, yes. We met a few weeks ago. Tell me, is there any word of Robyn?"

"No. Monsieur, we're scared to death. Gilly is at the KOMO television station. They are taping another plea for information. Oh, Monsieur, I'm so afraid for her. If anything should happen—"

"Nicole, I pray with you. Please tell Gillianne I inquired. I'll call again in the morning."

"Morning?"

"Yes, Mademoiselle. It is evening here in Paris."

"I'll tell her, Monsieur."

A commercial for dog food snapped on the screen replacing the sweet face of baby Robyn and her mother's pleas for anyone with information to call the tip line. Gabby quickly walked to Gilly's side, took her hand and led her from the bright lights of the television studio. The live telecast had been taped and would be aired every hour.

Gilly felt the vibration of her cell and pulled it from her suit pocket.

"Gilly, DuBois here. I only have a minute but wanted to tell you the dog found a white baby's sock, pink lace on top. Sound familiar?"

"Yes, yes. She had those little socks on. Her fa … yes."

"A few yards from the sock, my deputy also found cigarette butts. Lots of them in various stages of decomposition. I'd say the guy, I'm saying guy because we don't know if the kidnapper was male or female, had been there a long time. I don't mean just yesterday, but several days, weeks maybe. Because it rained the night before, the dirt next to the driveway of your neighbor … is the neighbor home to the north of your grandfather's house?"

"No. They've been gone for several months. Why?"

"We found a tire print in the dirt to the side of their driveway— almost to the road but next to some bushes, same area as the butts. There were also a couple of footprints in the wet dirt, but only a couple—large, deep, probably a man's. My guy thinks he found another one about six feet from the other two, but in the leaves so it could be wishful thinking. That's it."

"Thanks, Detective. I just finished with another television interview. I—

"I saw you. Good job, Gilly. Keep getting the word out."

"I'm going back home, my apartment. Let me know if—

"Yeah, I will."

Chapter 32

The Turkish Airline flight from Istanbul to Paris touched down at Charles de Gaulle Airport at 10:40 p.m. It was ten minutes late.

The woman, clutching a fussy baby, followed the man off the plane. With the aid of escalators, elevators, and asking numerous questions on how to exit the airport and find a cab, the family was finally traveling the streets of Paris to the Verlain Hotel.

The weary travelers quickly checked in and were escorted to their room on the fourth floor. The man had informed the desk clerk that, even though it was late, he was expecting a visitor, a woman, sometime in the next hour and to please give her their room number.

Closing the door behind the bellman, the man looked around the small room. The walls were a pale yellow with blue, white, and yellow stripped drapes covering the only window. A bed, made up for sleeping, was pulled down from a wall pocket. An open door revealed a closet-sized bathroom.

The woman tried to calm the baby who was now very upset, screaming her head off, arms and legs shaking as she cried. Her little chin quivering with each scream.

The man fished out his cell phone and placed a call. He couldn't stand the screaming kid and hastily stepped out into the hall.

The woman fumbled with a water bottle trying to unscrew the nipple cap. She put a dash of the sedative mixture she had left into the water, returned the nipple, and shook the bottle. Satisfied she pushed the nipple into the baby's mouth. At first the baby screamed louder, then with a whimper she began to suck on the nipple and soon she fell fast asleep.

Exhausted, the woman laid the baby on the couch placing a pillow along her side to keep her from falling to the floor.

The man returned to the room, frowned looking at the sleeping baby.

"Did you reach her?" the woman asked the man.

"Yes. She should be here any minute. You let me do the talking. Always stand in front of the kid. Do not, I repeat, do not let her pick up that baby until I say so. No money—no baby. We can't be too careful."

They both jerked at the sound of the soft knock on the door.

"Okay, here we go. Remember, do not let her pick up the baby."

"For God's sake open the door will ya? I know what to do. You just be sure you get the dough."

The man opened the door and a fashionably dressed blond woman stepped into the room, looked around, and spotted the baby. "So, you finally did what I hired you to do," the woman said in a soft, sarcastic voice. "Took you long enough." She looked around the room again and immediately stepped to the couch, bending over to pick up the sleeping infant.

The man's companion quickly interceded. "Oh no you don't, lady. Money first, then the baby. You can see from where you're standing that she's the one you wanted. Why, I don't know. Screamed the whole time. We should charge you double." She pulled a small wrinkled picture from her slacks pocket. "See. She's the one." A hoity-toity blonde, she thought. She sure needs a touch up appointment for that brassy blond hair.

The blonde opened her purse, retrieved an envelope and handed it to the man. Turning, she again tried to pick up the sleeping infant.

"You're a sly one. Back up. Let him count it. Wouldn't want you to short change us."

The man nodded. "Okay. It's all here. Let her have the kid."

The blonde picked up the baby. Took the diaper bag from the woman's outstretched hand and quickly left.

It was now close to one a.m.

Chapter 33

Unable to sleep, Maxime threw the covers to the end of the bed and twisted to sit on the edge. He glanced at the clock. 5:30 a.m.

He grasped the remote and switched on the television. Was there any news about the kidnapping of his baby? He suffered through the weather report, Syrian slaughter continued, the stock market took another hit closing yesterday down two percent.

Switching off the television he padded into the bathroom hoping a steaming hot shower would wash away the tension building in his body. Standing under the showerhead, eyes closed, the water beating down, he realized the tension his body was not abating. His hope of soothing his nerves had not worked.

Picking up a fluffy white bath towel, he vigorously rubbed his body—head, shoulders, back—then secured the towel around his waist and returned to the bedroom. A hot mug of coffee was on his dresser. Eric must have heard the shower running, he thought. Thank God for Eric, his trusted friend and valet. He had served Maxime since the day Maxime joined his grandfather's firm over ten years ago.

He sipped the coffee, instead of jolting his system awake, the shock of hot liquid relaxed his nerves. Dressing, he looked into the mirror while fastening his cufflinks. He was not going to the Senate today. Maybe later he'd go to his office at the law firm … no, he had to stay home … wait for word, any word of Robyn's whereabouts … had to be here for Gillianne.

Throwing his tie on the bed, he bent down to slip on his shoes when he heard a commotion. It came from the living room. With a sharp wrap on his bedroom door the door burst open. Bernadette marched up to him and deposited a very upset baby wrapped in a blanket into his arms.

"Now what have you done?" Maxime said. Carefully removing the blanket from the baby's head, he looked down in disbelief. Robyn?

She let out a scream as if her soft red curls were on fire. Her face contorted and red from crying, her eyes pinched shut, Maxime hugged the infant to his chest, his eyes filling with tears.

Eric ran into the room. "Monsieur, I'm so sorry. Madame insisted—"

"It's okay, Eric. Call my doctor. Tell him it's an emergency. I need him right away."

Maxime began to pace slowly around his bedroom gently patting Robyn's back, trying to calm her. Bernadette stood leaning against the doorjamb, a triumphant smile on her face. It was obvious to her that Maxime knew what he held in his arms.

"I give you what you want, Maxime. We are now a family. The Beaumont bloodline continues. You needn't fret over how you will care for the baby. I've instructed Eric to have my things returned here … to our apartment—

Maxime's mind was spinning. Little Robyn safe in his arms. A miracle. She stopped crying pushing her curls under his chin, began sucking her thumb. He had to call Gillianne immediately. But first he had to deal with the psychotic woman standing in the doorway of his bedroom.

"How did you get her?" he whispered in a menacing voice.

She ignored his ill temper. "Oh, well, it took quite awhile. But … well … once she was born I figured you, and yes the Count, the poor dear thinking his illustrious family would end with you, Maxime, would move heaven and earth to claim the child. So you see, my dear husband—

"You are no longer my wife, Bernadette."

"Technicality. You're a lawyer, a Senator. You can fix that with a stroke of a pen. Nobody really knows about the divorce anyway. Friends think I just had a nervous breakdown and needed to get away to regain my health."

"How did you get her?" Maxime hissed again in a whisper.

"Does it really matter? You have your precious bastard child—oh, we'll tell everyone that I went away to have the baby. It was just too stressful here in Paris, that you were afraid for my wellbeing and—

"Monsieur, your doctor will be here shortly."

Maxime strode out of the bedroom holding his precious baby tight to his chest, passed Bernadette, and told Eric to follow. Now several paces away from his ex-wife, Maxime whispered to Eric to call the police. Tell them to come immediately, that a kidnapper is in the apartment, but no sirens or she might flee.

Eric's brows shot up, his eyes wide darting from his employer to Bernadette. He turned and walked quickly from the room.

Robyn consoled, snuggled deeper into her father's arms an occasional hiccup from crying jolting her little body. Maxime looked at Bernadette lounging on the dark red velvet couch, one hand on the arm, her other relaxed on the back.

I have to keep her here, Maxime thought, as he continued to slowly stroll around the living room with Robyn. He paused at the window overlooking the Seine and the street below. A police vehicle pulled to a stop in front of the building. Three officers sprang out disappearing through the entrance.

Eric was waiting at the door. All the officers knew was what they were told about a call for help. That Senator Beaumont's ex-wife had arrived with a baby and that the Senator said he was detaining a kidnapper. The officers entered the foyer and Eric nodded for them to proceed into the living room.

"Senator Beaumont." The officer nodded to Maxime. "What's the situation, Monsieur?"

"This woman, Bernadette Beaumont, my *ex-wife*, kidnapped this baby in the States, from her mother Gillianne Wilder. This is the kidnapped infant who's been in the news the last few hours, days."

"Are you charging her with kidnapping, Monsieur?" the officer asked.

"Yes. Arrest her. Get her out of here."

"We'll take her to the department, detain her, keep her under arrest while we sort this out. Someone will be in touch with you today. We'll take your statement as to the charges. Come with us, Madame Beaumont."

"What? Surely you aren't taking his word for this. He's the one who ordered the kidnapping."

Two officers, one on either side, physically lifted her under her arms and half dragged her out of the apartment.

"He's the baby's father," she screamed over her shoulder. "You can't do this. Take your hands off me."

Eric shut the door muffling her screams. Shaking his head he looked at Maxime.

"Eric, please call my mother. She's at the country villa. Tell her I need her help and show the doctor in as soon as he gets here. I want him to check the baby immediately to be sure she hasn't been harmed."

Maxime carried Robyn back to his bedroom, laid her on the bed, and reached for the phone. Looking at the clock, he knew it was approaching midnight in Seattle.

"Gillianne Wilder."

"Gillianne, I have her," Maxime said in a joyful whisper.

"Maxime. What did you say?"

"My darling, Robyn is laying on the bed ... in my bedroom ... Paris."

"But ... how? Maxime," Gilly yelled into the phone. "Did you take her?"

"No, no, no. The kidnapper brought her to me. She is safe, Gillianne. The kidnapper has been arrested ... taken to a Paris jail."

"Maxime, ... what ... I don't understand ... what are you saying? Are you sure she's okay?" Gilly sounded hysterical trying to grasp his words.

"She's lying here like a little red-haired angel. My doctor is coming to the apartment—there's the bell. He must be here."

Maxime heard her sniffle, gulping for air.

"Gillianne, please don't cry. Our baby is safe. The doctor is here. I will call you back as soon as he examines her. But my darling, Robyn is safe. Do you hear me?"

"Yes. Robyn's alive," she whispered.

"I will explain what I know when I call back which isn't much. The only thing I know for certain is that she brought her to me."

"She?"

"Bernadette ... my ex-wife."

Chapter 34

Seattle

Gilly sat in the dark on the edge of her bed, the light of the moon cascading over the bed covers. She laid her head in her hands and began sobbing. Nicole and Gabby heard her and raced from their bedrooms to her side. They feared the worse—Robyn was dead. Patting Gilly's arm, Nicole reached for the tissue box on the bedside table, plucked a tissue and pushed it into Gilly's hand.

Feeling the tissue, Gilly raised her head, a smile spreading across her tear-stained face, gasping for air, sobs catching in her throat. Nicole and Gabby exchanged surprised looks.

"What happened, Gilly?" Nicole asked.

"Maxime called."

"Maxime?" Gabby said her brows now furrowed with renewed alarm.

"He has Robyn. She's safe."

"But … how?" Nicole asked, tears of relief springing to her eyes. She plucked two tissues another for Gilly and one for herself.

"All he said was that his ex-wife brought Robyn to him. She's been arrested and he was waiting for a doctor to examine Robyn."

"What does that mean?" Gabby asked. "Is she hurt?"

"I don't think so. He said he'd call me back as soon as the doctor left." Gilly reached for her bottle of water next to the tissue box and took several swallows.

"It's midnight in Paris," Nicole said glancing at the clock. "How about Gabby and I wait here with you? Wait for Maxime to call."

Gilly nodded in agreement and the three women squirmed under the covers, Gabby and Nicole on their backs staring at the ceiling, Gilly on her side staring at the clock.

Chapter 35

Paris

The doctor removed the syringe from Robin's arm filled with her blood. "Look at that he said," smiling as he swabbed the puncture with gauze. "Not a whimper. "I'll take this to the lab right away just to make sure she doesn't have anything toxic in her system. Other than that I think you'd better feed the poor thing. If I'm not mistaken that quivering little lip is asking to be fed. Do you have something to give her? Do you know what she generally has—milk or perhaps a little cereal as well?"

Relieved that the doctor found nothing, Maxime picked up the little girl, holding her head back a little from his chest, she patted his chin and then began to cry, scrunching her red face into a mass of tears.

"I'll call her mother right away and find out. Also, my mother should be here shortly to give me a hand."

"Good, I think you're going to need a little help in the baby department," the doctor said chuckling as he packed his bag to leave. "Although, you seem to have the situation in hand so far. I'll call you with the results of the blood test—probably late this afternoon."

"Thank you, doctor. If you'll excuse me I'd like to call her mother."

"Go right ahead, Senator. By the way, where did the child get those red curls? It surely wasn't from you."

Maxime laughed. "From her mother."

As the doctor left the bedroom, Maxime cradled the crying infant. "There, there, ma chérie, I'll call your mama right now. Find out what I can feed you."

Gilly picked up the phone before the first ring ended. "Maxime, what did the doctor say. She's crying. I can hear her."

"He said she's hungry, my darling. Quickly, tell me what I can feed our daughter."

He laid Robyn on the bed so he could write down how much milk, water, yes, a little cereal. As he was taking notes his mother ran into the room and quickly took charge of the red-faced baby, cooing to her as she carried her out of the bedroom.

"Maxime, what just happened? She's not crying. I can't hear her. Maxime—

"Everything is fine, sweetheart. My mother just picked her up. Do all you mothers know instantly what to do with a crying baby? Hold on a minute."

Eric poked his head into the bedroom and Maxime handed him the scribbled notes, told him to give the notes to the Countess and to go get whatever she says fast.

"We're getting things under control, my darling."

"Maxime, how did Bernadette get—

"I don't know yet. All she told me was that she knew about the baby and thought if she gave her to me that we would be a family, that I'd take her back. I don't know how she managed to do it. She must have hired someone, but I don't know who or how."

"Maxime, how soon can you bring Robyn to me? Can you fly out—

"Gillianne, my darling, please listen to me. I beg you to come to Paris. Give me, my mother and father a few days with our baby. Just a few days, that's all I ask. We can stay at the family's villa in the country. I grew up there ... I want you to learn of my family ... like I understood more about you when I visited your family, your wonderful grandfather. Please, Gillianne, will you come here? I promise as soon as you want to return home I will help you. Will you?"

Maxime waited for her reply. He was afraid the line had been disconnected, but then he heard her answer, a whisper.

"Yes, I'll come to Paris. As soon as I know my flight numbers I'll call you. And, Maxime, guard Robyn with your life."

"Oh, I will, my precious. We will meet you at the airport. The moment you land you will see us and you will hold Robyn again."

Chapter 36

Hansville

Skip turned down Gramp's driveway and parked. He sat, thoughts of Gilly and Robyn running through his head. Agatha gave him a slurp on the cheek. "Okay, Aggie. Let's go." With a sigh, Skip opened the car door and Agatha quickly jumped down, ran to the patio with a howl.

"Hey, anybody home?"

"Back here, Skip. In the kitchen," Gramps called out.

Skip strode down the hall and the two men locked their blue eyes. Skip walked to the old man, put his arms around him. "Robyn's safe," Skip said. Releasing Gramps he turned to the stove and poured the boiling water over the teabags in the two mugs that Gramps had set out.

"Do you know Gilly's on her way to Paris to bring Robyn home?" Gramps asked.

"Yeah. Nicole called me. What do you think about the fact that she turns up with her father? Looks to me like he planned the whole thing."

"I met him a few weeks ago," Gramps said taking a sip of tea that Skip had placed in front of him.

Skip's head jerked up. "Here?"

"Yup. Seems he flew to Seattle to see his baby. Gilly brought him over to meet us."

"What? *She* brought him here?"

"Well, it wasn't quite like that … she wasn't anxious to bring him across the sound. Anne and Will were here—had lunch."

Skip couldn't sit. He stood. Walked to the window over the sink, stared out the little window questioning what Gramps said. What the heck is going on? Seems everyone is cozy with this guy and I didn't even know he'd met them. Face it, Hunter, you're losing her to the seducer. How long is it going to take for her to learn what a creep he is?

Skip turned to Gramps. "What did you think of him?"

"He's haunted."

"Haunted? Come on, Clay."

"Skip, all I know is that Gilly went to Paris to bring Robyn home. You can't jump to conclusions. Wait 'til she gets back."

"Wait! I'm doing a lot of that lately. Did she tell you I was thinking about writing a story about a double blackmail?"

"Not that I recall. You mean a story about Edward Churchill? If you're talking double blackmail then the second part of that story would be about Robyn's father, Maxime Beaumont."

"Bingo! My idea really set Gilly off. I didn't approach it right. Shouldn't have said anything."

"Well, it's probably good that you did. Now you know how she feels about the idea. Sometimes an idea isn't worth pursuing."

"You got that right," Skip said turning back to look out the window over the sink. The neighbor's blinds were shut. "It's tricky, writing about events that deal with people you know. Wellington wanted some major edits to the gold robbery. A story seems to get tangled up with people's emotions."

"Sounds like you have lots of questions whirling around in that head of yours, son. If you feel a story is worth telling, then you have to write it and live with the consequences if you bring in people you know, care about."

Skip sighed. "I'd better go run. Clear my head."

"Sometimes that's hard to do—clear it—until you can answer some of the questions residing there. Come up with some answers … then let the questions go," Gramps said.

Skip smiled. "Week eight. Half way through my training schedule. Fourteen miles today. Maybe I'll come up with some answers if the strain doesn't kill me first."

"You'll be okay. I'll have lunch ready for you."

Skip strode out to do his stretching routine, then began his run at a slow pace to warm up.

His next three hours were hard.

He couldn't concentrate. He wanted to work on his mental imaging, his focus so complete that running felt good, time would flow by, his feet flying over the pavement. But it wasn't working for him today. His conversation with Gramps raised concern over what Gilly was doing in Paris. Over that Beaumont guy again taking advantage of her, maybe to the point of kidnapping.

"In. In. In.

"Out.

"In." He shouted.

"Shit. I can't even breathe right."

He slowed to a walk. Drank eight ounces of Gatorade.

The motorcycle couple shot by him, waving.

"Sure, now you wave. I make a fool of myself telling DuBois you kidnapped Robyn and now you wave."

He picked up his pace.

"Have to start cross training this week. Go to the gym. Work on the quads, biceps, upper body," he said to a flock of seagulls overhead.

Returning to Gramp's house three hours later, he flopped in the kitchen chair. He never felt so tired after a run. Ate half of his sandwich. Finished the cup of tea. Both Agatha and Coco sat in the doorway watching him.

"Gramps, I'm pooped. Think I'll go on back to Seattle."

"Oh? No writing this weekend?"

"Maybe back at my condo. I want to go to the gym … do some training with the free weights." Skip put his plate in the dishwasher. "Thanks for listening to my babble. I'll see you next week."

Chapter 37

Beaumont Country Villa

Paris

The plane circled over the twinkling lights of Paris, 8:10 p.m. Gazing out the window, Gilly thought back four years earlier when she eagerly took her first steps into the next phase of learning about the business of fashion design from where the industry was born—the city of lights. Butterflies raised havoc in her stomach then and butterflies of a different sort were at it now.

She yearned to hold Robyn, to kiss her pink cheeks, but she knew some of those butterflies were in anticipation of seeing Maxime … here in Paris … the city she didn't think she'd ever see again. She didn't know what to expect, how she was going to feel seeing him once more where they had shared the first blush of passion. The return ticket was burning a hole in her shoulder bag.

Five days in Paris ... with him ... meeting his family.

Gilly sighed. I can make it through five days, she thought. A smile crossed her face. "Robyn, mommy's coming, she whispered to her reflection in the window as the plane pulled up to the gate. "Just a few more minutes, my little angel."

Gilly pressed forward in the crowd, navigating around sleepy passengers plodding their way to the baggage carousels. Breaking free of the line, her eyes scanning the people standing outside of the rope, she saw him. Oh God, he was holding Robyn so her little face, her eyes were looking right at her. Gilly ran dragging her rolling suitcase. She ducked under the rope, dropped her suitcase handle and ran to the infant. Her eyes only on her child, she lifted her from Maxime's arms, cradled her, kissed her, stroking her curls and laughing as tears rolled down her face. Robyn's little arms circled her mother's neck in a tight hug.

Maxime retrieved her suitcase, put his arm around Gilly and gently guided her to the parking garage. Thirty minutes later, Maxime at the wheel of his silver Peugeot was driving them through the streets of Paris. He circled around the Eiffel Tower, then down the Champs-Elysées. Glancing at Gillianne, he was happy to see her eagerly twisting and turning at the sights she had grown to love during the brief period she was in Paris before. Delighted at scenes passing her window, she turned to see what Robyn thought of all the lights but she was sound asleep in her carrier.

"You must be exhausted, Gillianne. I hope you don't mind if we go straight to my parent's country home."

"I never want to sleep again. I'm so thankful to have Robyn back." Gilly twisted again to look at the sleeping baby, smiling she turned to the front and Maxime took her hand as she leaned back in her seat, kissing her knuckles and returning her hand to her lap.

He kept telling himself to move slowly, try to win her heart with loving support—watch out for the kisses. Give her time, he thought.

The silver car sped out of the city into the country—glimpses of fields, trees and bushes caught in the car's headlights. He kept glancing at her out of the corners of his eyes. She was beginning to relax. He couldn't believe she was in the car with him ... he could reach out and touch her ... she was so close. His little family together. No! Don't let your mind go there, he thought. It was enough for the moment that she was here in Paris, here sitting beside him.

Turning down a country lane the trees parted revealing a large vine covered house, beige stucco and pinkish-grey slate roof, beautiful and mellow with age. Every window shining brightly with lamps turned on welcoming her.

Gilly turned and laughed. "Little country villa?"

Maxime smiled at her. "I guess it's not quite little, but you will find it homey."

The door flew open, a splash of light falling on the old stone steps and a woman, her black hair with wisps of gray drawn back into a bun, stepped out and waved to them.

"That's my mother, you'll like her—very warm and understanding."

"What do I call her … Countess? Madame Beaumont—

"I asked her that. Her name is Madeleine and her friends call her Maddy. She said she wants to be your friend." Maxime smiled easily. He was looking forward to showing Gillianne his boyhood home and especially the warm welcome he knew awaited her.

His father had melted when he first caught sight of Robyn. Maxime had to practically pry her out of his father's arms. Neither man spoke about how different things would have been if the Count's detective had been successful in eliminating the mother with child. They agreed that that harrowing thought was to be buried so deep that it would never be spoken or thought of again. Truth be told, the Count was so distraught after seeing Robyn and the possibility that her life might have ended in the womb, that he had become a major supporter of the little Catholic church in the village center a few miles from where his villa stood. He hadn't been able to bring himself to a full confession of what he had done, attempted to do, but he hoped to somehow redeem himself in the eyes of God, his family, and his precious granddaughter.

Maxime ambled to the other side of the car, removed Robyn from her car seat and placed her in Gillianne's outstretched arms. The baby snuggled her head under Gilly's chin, her thumb in her mouth and the other little hand patting her mother's cheek. Maxime retrieved the slightly worn white bunny from the car and tucked it under Robyn's arm automatically drawing the stuffed animal tight to her body.

"Mother, I'd like you to meet Gillianne Wilder. Gillianne, my mother, Madeleine."

"I'm so happy to meet you, Gillianne," the woman said kissing both of Gilly's cheeks and giving a tender pat on Robyn's red curls. "Come in, please. I'll show you where the kitchen is in the event you need something during the night."

Madeleine led the way to a big kitchen with copper pots hanging from a wrought iron pot rack and colorful pottery lined up in an old cherry breakfront buffet. White lace curtains framed the windows drawn back with green ribbon. The small window panes were made of old glass. Wide, well worn floorboards were polished to a lustrous sheen.

"There are three baby bottles of milk and two with water in the refrigerator," Madeleine explained as she walked around the kitchen ... everything ready for Robyn's return since she left with her father to go to the airport.

"Now, let's go upstairs to your bedroom. You must be very tired. I had a crib set up in your room. I thought you might like Robyn to be in with you, but—"

"That sounds perfect, thank you."

Maxime was standing at the bottom of the stairs, his body relaxed, face serene for the first time since he realized what a fool he had been to let Gillianne flee from his life. She was here in his boyhood home, the place where the outside world and all that ailed it, ceased to exist. "I put your suitcase in the bedroom. Sleep well." He kissed her cheek, then Robyn's and stepped back as Gillianne followed his mother up the stairs.

Gilly paused on the top step to look at him once more. "Thank you, Maxime."

Madeleine pushed open a tongue-and-groove paneled door, its rich patina soft to the eye. Gilly stepped into the bedroom—a room she had only dreamed of in pictures. The white embroidered canopy over the antique four-poster bed was made up with a colorful patchwork quilt. It too showed its age with a fray here and there from loving use over the years. The crib beside the bed was covered with a matching baby quilt. Gilly couldn't have felt more honored— she was allowed to see pieces of life that had existed in this home over many decades.

"You can open the windows if you like although the night air is a bit chilly this time of year. There's a bathroom across the hall. It's all yours. Is there anything else you might need?"

Gilly laid the sleeping baby in the crib, pulled the quilt up under her chin and looked down marveling that she could once again touch her.

"Get up whenever you like," Madeleine said with an easy smile. "Although I guess the little one will let you know when it's time. I want to thank you, Gillianne, for giving my husband and me a few days to get to know you and your beautiful baby."

Gilly turned, smiling.

"Gilly, please call me Gilly," Gilly said in a whisper.

"Then you must call me Maddy, dear." Maddy gave Gilly a quick hug and turned to leave.

"Thank you, Maddy ... for everything."

The two women looked into each other's eyes, understanding and cherishing their special bond. Smiling, Maddy softly closed the door behind her.

Chapter 38

The country kitchen was warm and cozy in the soft glow of the recessed lighting under the cabinets. Gilly opened her mouth so Robyn would mimic her as she slid the last spoon of baby cereal into her mouth. Wiping her chin and cooing what a good girl she was, Gilly lifted her from the highchair, picked up the baby bottle with a few drops of milk left and padded back to her bedroom. Robyn was asleep before the last of the bottle was gone, and Gilly laid her in the crib.

The sun was rising revealing a beautiful, cloudless sky as Gilly snuggled back under the down comforter falling asleep as quickly as Robyn.

Hearing conversation outside, Gilly glanced at the clock—she had slept two hours. Glancing at Robyn and seeing she was still asleep, Gilly retrieved her black slacks from the chair and a fresh white long-sleeved white blouse from the top of her suitcase. She finished dressing and quickly tied her long hair with a black ribbon at the nape of her neck. Pushing her feet into her black flats, she left the bedroom quietly closing the door. Pausing to put on silver hoop earrings she then scampered down the stairs and out the French doors to a flagstone patio.

Shielding her eyes from the sun, she saw Maddy across an expanse of lawn painting at an easel which stood outside an open barn door. A bouquet of colorful mums in a cobalt-blue vase sat on a white lace doily to the side of the easel. Smiling, Maddy waved to her and motioned for her to come over.

Gilly looked up at her bedroom window, wondering, then crossed the grass to Maddy's side.

"I've asked Gertie to come meet you as soon as she sees you're up. She'll let us know if she hears Robyn, actually she'll keep checking on her. She's been thrilled to have a baby in the house. Are you comfortable having Gertie on the lookout?" Maddy asked.

"Yes, and thanks. She was sleeping soundly, but you never know."

"Did you see the intercom by the crib? I left it on all the time. We weren't taking any chances on not hearing her."

"I did see it. Is there a speaker out here?" Gilly asked.

"There, on the barn door. It's turned up to full blast," Maddy said laughing.

Gilly stood looking at the painting on the easel. "Very pretty ... I can see the morning sun on the petals."

Maddy nodded her head to go into the barn. "Help yourself to coffee. It's probably stronger than you like. I usually have a shot of espresso to get me going in the morning."

Gilly returned and sat on an old weather-beaten chair a few feet from where Maddy was painting. Maddy wiped off her brush, picked up her coffee cup and sat on a matching chair beside Gilly. Both women stretched their legs out in front of them, raising their faces to the warmth of the sun's rays.

"Maddy, you really are an artist. The barn, if you can call it that with the white-washed wood, your gallery?"

"Yes. Painting keeps me centered. It's so peaceful here compared to the city. We're spending more and more time out here. Blackie began to change a few months ago. Slowed down."

"Blackie?"

"Maxime's father. A nickname from his grade school days—his big black eyes. I'm about the only one who calls him that now. Anyway, we're spending more and more time here in the country away from the law firm. He loves his horses, riding and grooming them. Something he used to leave to his property manager. But when he caught sight of Robyn, his granddaughter," she whispered. "Well, the change became more dramatic. Overnight really. In the last twenty-four hours I've caught him wiping tears from his eyes as he waited for Maxime to bring the baby and you to our home."

"Are you worried about his health?"

"I wasn't at first—the change happened slowly. I did call his doctor and he told me that his last checkup showed nothing but a very healthy man. But that checkup was over six months ago. And then suddenly, in the last few weeks, he lost weight. He's a skeleton of the man he was at your age. I catch him staring off into space. I don't know what he sees or what's going on behind that blank stare. When I ask what's bothering him he doesn't answer me."

They fell silent in the warmth of the sun, Gilly's eyes following the lines of the flowerbeds, not manicured as the gardens in the Paris parks, but casual, inviting. You could pick one of the flowers and not feel like you'd get your hand slapped.

"Blackie started to change at the same time Maxime changed." Maddy picked up the conversation where she'd left off. "It was as if they shifted positions. Come to think of it, they changed about the time Maxime learned you had given birth to a baby girl. Blackie must have known about you, but I didn't. When Maxime came to me, told me about you, I was furious with him. So angry at how he had treated you."

Gilly squinted, sat up straight looking at Maddy. This sophisticated, beautiful woman was sharing her private thoughts, talking through what had happened over the year. She was revealing her love for her husband and her son and how she felt powerless to help them when, to her, they needed her the most.

"But Maxime ... " she looked over at Gilly. "I saw a man torn up inside. He shouldn't have been. He had won the Senate seat—a seat Blackie had groomed him for. But it didn't seem to matter. Oh, he attacked his new duties, does a good job in my estimation, but the light was gone from his eyes. It wasn't long after that that he divorced Bernadette. Banished her from their Paris apartment. He was generous seeing that she had a house in the south and the money to handle it. Although Bernadette never had enough money." Maddy chuckled. "Blackie and I spoke many times over the years about what a mistake we had made pushing those two into marriage. A loveless marriage."

Gilly reached out, touched Maddy's arm. "You did what you thought best. Don't beat yourself up over things past. From the looks of the man, I'd say you and Blackie did a good job," Gilly said smiling.

Maddy laid her hand on Gilly's and then both women leaned back in their chairs. "You are very wise for your age, Gillianne."

"That's more my Gramps talking. He has a way of setting me straight," Gilly said with a soft chuckle.

"Thank you, dear. I feel our family is close for the first time." Maddy gazed at Gilly. "Family. I haven't thought of that word for years. Seeing Blackie and our son holding ... Robyn, oh my, I feel we are a family. You've given us ... these few days mean so much. Thank you again, Gilly. And now before I start blubbering, I'd better get back to my painting. I see that son of mine heading our way."

Chapter 39

Maxime strode across the lawn to the two women with a happy baby in his arms. Both watched him approach—one seeing her beloved son, the other seeing a strapping man nine years her senior, dressed in jeans, white shirt with his sleeves rolled up bearing down on her with their baby, her heart skipping a beat.

"I'm not sure it's a good idea to leave you two alone together," he said smiling as he kissed his mother's cheek and throwing caution to the wind kissing Gilly's hand then her cheek.

Gilly opened her arms accepting the handoff, bouncing Robyn on her knee.

Maxime stood towering over her with his hands on his hips. "Don't think you're going to spend this beautiful day watching my mother paint. I've asked Gertie—

"Gertie?" Gilly stood shading her eyes with her hand.

"I think he's talking about her job of overseeing all things kitchen related," Maddy answered enjoying the by-play between the two.

"She's packing a little picnic for us. Two picnic baskets that will fit strapped to the handlebars of our bikes."

"Our bikes?"

"God, woman, you ask a lot of questions. Mother will you look after Robyn for a couple of hours while I show this young lady the lake that happens to be on our property?"

"Oh, no," Gilly said alarmed.

"Don't worry, dear. I promise she'll be with me every minute. And if we both want a nap, I'll lay down on your bed … if that's all right with you?"

Gilly looked from Maddy to Maxime and back to his mother. She looked down at her shoe, then up again at Maddy. "Of course, it's all right. And thank you."

"Then it's settled," Maxime said pulling Gilly to her feet. "But you have to help me drag the bicycles out of the barn. They haven't been ridden for years. Mother, do you have a pair of jeans Gillianne can borrow because we're going to have to wash the bikes?"

"Sure. Gilly, come with me and if that son of mine is talking about washing those bikes then that means he's going to drag the hose out. Let's take Robyn inside with us."

Maxime watched as they disappeared through the French doors. Those are the three most precious women in my life, he thought. Take it slow. She didn't pull away when your lips touched her skin just now.

Maxime shook his head and entered the back of the barn to find the bicycles.

Gilly returned in green shorts, white shirt with tails tied in front, and a pair of white sandals. Maxime had the hose on, rinsing off the lady's bike, and threw her a wet soapy sponge. "Here, you go wipe them down with the sponge and I'll—

"Oh, no you don't. I'll get the hose." She threw the wet sponge back at him, hitting him in the chest, and grabbed for the hose.

Surprised at the sponge he lifted the hose as she went to grab it giving her a face full of cold water.

"Hey, that's not fair," she squealed. Now holding the hose she let him have it as he turned his back to her receiving the full force of the water on his back.

Laughing he raised his hands. "I give up. Stop. Stop."

"Okay, but now you get to work with that sponge. Don't think I'm going to spend this *beautiful* day washing bikes. I thought you said something about a picnic."

Bikes washed, wet clothes exchanged for dry jeans, T-shirts, and sneakers, Maxime and Gilly pedaled down a country path dotted with wild flowers and lined with trees. He led her to a clearing bordering a small lake with a large stand of trees on the other side.

Gilly held the handlebars of the bikes while Maxime removed the picnic baskets. Laying the bikes to the side, they opened the baskets and spread out Gertie's idea of a picnic next to a large tree—tablecloth, bottle of wine, crystal glasses, sandwiches of butter, ham and cheese on a fresh baguette, salad greens and strawberry tartelettes.

Gilly looked over the spread. "Where do you find a Gertie?"

"Hey, I can't tell you all the family secrets on your first picnic," he said. Picking up the corkscrew, he nodded to show her Gertie thought of everything, and opened then poured the wine into the glasses Gilly was holding.

He handed her one of the sandwiches and a tart. Gilly leaned against the tree, sipping her wine, then took a bite of her sandwich. It was so thick she had a hard time and ended up pulling it apart. "You're not playing fair you know," she said gazing out at the water. "And you know what I'm talking about."

"I know." He had planned this picnic in the hope she would remember the one he had spread out for her high on the hills of Monaco overlooking the Mediterranean Sea. This little lake wasn't the Mediterranean, but the passion he felt for her that day didn't come close to matching the depth of his love for her today. "Do you mind?"

She didn't answer him, kept gazing at the water. "It's lovely here. Is this where you swam as a little boy?"

"Yes. Me and some friends. Usually my mother knew, but not always. Sometimes I'd sneak out at night."

"Oh, oh. I bet you were a handful. You and your friends."

"My friends, yes. Me … not so much. My father … well, he ruled the roost, so to speak."

My father, he thought. I have to tell her what he did, what I didn't stop until later. Thank God it wasn't too late. Tell her … not today. Tomorrow.

Topping off their wine he asked her how the business was doing now that the shop had reopened. She asked him what being a senator was like, did he enjoy it, was he still active in the family law firm. The afternoon flew by—casual, comfortable conversation. Everything he hoped it would be.

Riding back home he led her to the village square. Maddy had told her about a September festival to be held in the square the day after tomorrow, the night before she left. She thought it might be fun for the whole family to go, have dinner there.

Gilly asked if there was a clothing shop in town. She wanted to buy a skirt and blouse for the festival. Maddy told her there would be music and dancing similar to a square dance in the States—slow dancing mixed with fast polkas. Maxime knew just the place but he wasn't sure if a fashion designer would be happy with the selection.

Gilly modeled a couple of skirts for Maxime performing the model catwalk. Laughing she quickly selected an ankle length, green-striped full skirt with an off-the-shoulder white embroidered peasant blouse. He divided her packages into the picnic baskets and then led the way home.

Dinner was lively. Maddy suggested they eat in the kitchen on the old pine harvest table. She invited Gertie to join them and Maxime produced two bottles of red wine to go along with Gertie's pork tenderloin she had sautéed with apples, and served with a brandy cream sauce.

Settling Robyn in her highchair, Gilly cornered Maddy, asking how she should address Maxime Beaumont Senior. Maddy suggested Blackie. She said she had talked to her husband while they were waiting for Maxime to bring her home from the airport. The Count thought Blackie was a splendid idea.

Gertie kept everyone laughing with her tales of her initial job as a cook—starting a grease fire in the oven the first time she roasted a duck, curdling a cream filling for the French Pastries, and dropping a serving dish of green beans almandine at a fancy dinner.

Maxime asked Robyn if she would like some cheese, serving her a sliver. She gummed it and then pointed to the cheese, "some."

"Um," Gilly said. "Quite a vocabulary—mama, dada, and some."

Maxime's heart quickened. He had taught her to say dada the few days before Gilly arrived. He was apprehensive, but Gilly had taken it in stride when she first heard Robyn say dada at the airport.

Blackie ate most of his dinner, didn't say anything unless Maddy asked him a question, and looked from one to the other as they jabbered. He smiled, however, at Robyn and *some* cheese.

After dinner, Maddy insisted on helping Gertie with the cleanup. Gilly started to clear the table when Robyn began whimpering, her face turning red, working up to a big cry. Cheese or not, she was hungry for her bottle and it was time for bed. By the time Gilly came back downstairs, Maxime had a fire blazing in the old stone fireplace, and Blackie was sitting in his leather wingchair, staring into the flames.

"Do you play checkers, Gilly?" Maddy asked sitting on the couch facing the fire. "I warn you though, Maxime was the neighborhood champ when he was a boy. However, he's probably a bit rusty now."

"Bring it on, Monsieur Neighborhood Bully. I happen to be the champ in my house unless Gramps is tired of letting me win."

The score at three games each, Maxime grinned at Gilly. "How about a tiebreaker?"

"Name it?" Gilly said, grinning back.

"A game of chess."

"Oh, well, chess is not exactly my cup of tea," she said fanning her face with her hand and feigning that she just might condescend to play a game.

"You're on, Madame."

An hour passed and Maddy and Blackie excused themselves. Maddy smiled to herself as she and Blackie strolled down the hall arm-in-arm. "Looks like a match made in heaven," she said.

"Yes, she seems to be a superb chess player."

"That's not what I meant and you know it," Maddy said squeezing her husband's arm.

The following day passed like the day before. Maxime and Gilly road their bikes to the village and watched the townspeople scurrying around preparing for the festival. A large white tent with a pointed top was raised on poles leaving the sides open. Squares of flooring were locked in place creating a surface strong enough to withstand the anticipated stomping of wild polkas. Long tables were tucked around with chairs and a platform setup for the musicians.

Spotting a little boy with an ice cream cone, Maxime whispered in Gilly's ear that they should go home and get Robyn. Gilly checked her watch, Robyn should be up from her nap. They pedaled furiously racing each other back to the villa. Maxime put the bikes away while Gilly went in the house to get Robyn. She found her in the kitchen with Maddy and Gertie, grabbed her sweater off the back of the highchair, and picked her up. "We're off to get an ice cream cone. Want anything?" she asked giggling as she tickled Robyn's tummy.

"No, run along. How's everybody doing in the village?"

"Pandemonium, Madame Maddy. Pandemonium."

Chapter 40

A warm September day enveloped the Paris countryside. At home, Gilly thought, we'd call it Indian summer. The household staff, Count and Countess, and by extension, Gilly and Maxime, were buzzing with preparations for the early evening festival.

Gertie had signed up to bring her special poached salmon in aspic dish topped with dollops of mayonnaise and ringed with lemon. Maxime was in charge of a tub of ice big enough to handle two large rectangular pottery dishes of the salmon. Blackie had several cases of wine delivered to the site—red and white from a vineyard near the village. Maxime contracted with the village baker to deliver various breads, enough for the entire festival.

Gilly modeled her skirt and blouse for Maddy, who took her by the hand to her bedroom and pulled out two eyelet petticoats from her closet. In her opinion, the striped skirt was in need of extra fullness underneath to be revealed when Gilly twirled around the dance floor. Maddy also retrieved a box wrapped in a pink bow pushing it into Gilly's hands. Opening the present, they both giggled over the green, footed rompers with a fuzzy white bunny covering the entire front. A green bonnet was in the bottom of the box. Maddy's excuse was that the evening was going to be chilly, so the child had to have something warm to wear. Well, didn't she?

The men weren't seen the entire day and Gertie would not allow Maddy and Gilly into her kitchen. If Robyn required feeding, they were to call on the intercom and the bottle of milk and whatever else they wanted appeared on the dining room table.

Blackie and Maddy left ahead of time so they could garner a table under the big tent to protect them from the sun and later should a cool breeze come up with the night air. Maxime delivered Gertie's offering under her scrutiny and constant barrage of orders to be careful.

Gilly and Robyn waited on the patio for Maxime to return from his salmon aspic delivery to escort them to the festival. He loaded a large stroller, with canopy, in the back of his car, but when he turned and saw Gillianne and Robyn sitting like princesses on the patio, he signaled for them to stay put. He dashed in the house, grabbed his camera, tickled Robyn's bunny tummy, and took several pictures of the gleeful pair.

Arriving at the festival, the little family was immediately surrounded by well wishers who wanted to meet the flaming redhead, and the baby with matching curls in the bunny suit. As prearranged, Maxime introduced Gillianne as Gillianne Wilder, a fashion designer, and her daughter Robyn who were visiting from the United States.

Big orange lanterns hung from the ceiling of the white tent enticing everyone to enter. The lines on either side of the food tables moved along quickly. First stop, salads of shredded carrots dressed in a vinaigrette, a salad of beans and onion came next, then Gertie's salmon.

Gilly looked up at Maxime, eyebrows raised at the next platter that looked like thinly sliced Prosciutto. He explained that it was called Jambon Cru, a French dry-cured ham. The meat was garnished with black olives, Gruyère cheese, cherry tomatoes, and miniature corn husks drizzled with olive oil and black pepper. Of course, Blackie's wine kept everyone in a festive mood. Later, trays of tarts, cookies and fruits were placed on the cleared tables, followed by coffee.

The musicians, two men wearing white shirts and black trousers, and a woman in a knee length blue dress, kept the crowd entertained. One man played a trumpet, the other played a red accordion, and the woman sang and tapped a tambourine in rhythm to the wild tunes mixed with lovely melodies flowing from under the tent. Children pretended to dance on the lawn outside the tent or tumbled in games of tag, while others blew bubbles through a wand.

Boyhood friends stopped to say hello to Maxime. One couple, who had shared several dinners with Maxime and Bernadette, asked about his ex-wife. They had read in the papers that she was arrested on kidnapping charges. Maxime told them that she was scheduled to be extradited to the States where the investigation was being vigorously pursued. He offered no further explanation, excusing himself to refill his father's wine glass.

As dusk descended, the muted light from the orange paper lanterns blended with tiny white lights giving the tent a hint of romance as the dancing began. Gilly followed Maxime easily with the slow dance but the polkas were more difficult. However, she soon got the hang of it flipping her skirt like a cabaret girl, her petticoats flying.

Gilly begged to sit a minute to catch her breath but one of Maxime's friends asked her to dance the next number which turned out to be a fast fox trot. Not to be out done, several other men asked the flaming redhead for a dance. Maddy saved her by waving her over to the table to take a rest. She and Blackie had had enough and, with Gilly's permission, were taking Robyn home to put the tired little girl to bed.

After helping his parents to the car, Maxime took Gilly's hand leading her to the dance floor as the musicians transitioned to a slow dance. When the music stopped the men held their partners wrapped in the mood of the warm night. The couples began drifting off the makeshift dance floor as the musicians left the stage for a much needed break.

"Can we go for a walk?" Maxime asked.

Gilly nodded in agreement and Maxime, grasping her hand, led her to a path bordered by the sweet scent of roses. They came to a bench nestled under a tree, the moon and stars visible through the branches.

"Did you enjoy yourself tonight?" Maxime asked. They both turned their backs to the corners of the bench so they faced each other.

"Oh, yes. You, Monsieur, couldn't walk two feet without someone greeting you, or asking questions. Did you know them all?"

"Some. They were *con…stit…u…ents*," he said laughing.

"I see. And did these *con…stit…u…ents* want something?"

"Always, my love, always."

Gilly leaned back gazing up at the stars.

"Gillianne, I've been putting off something I have to tell you. I must confess to you. These days with you have been so wonderful. I didn't want the time to ever end, but there are some things you don't know. Something my father did but I didn't stop him, and—"

Gilly could see Maxime's tortured face in the moonlight. "Surely, it can't be so bad. I—"

"At first I was too cowardly to stop him. Then I faced him. Demanded he stop the madness."

Gilly looked intently into Maxime's eyes trying to understand what he was saying.

He stood, walked to a tree a few feet away and then turned. "When I told my father I was being blackmailed because an American woman was pregnant with my child, he didn't believe me. He laughed. But when I told him it was possible he stopped laughing, became irate. He said if the information got into the media that I would lose the election. It was going to be close and this news could tip the scales. Gillianne, he … he … put out a contract on your life."

"What?" Gilly jumped from the bench, clenched her fists, head down, mind spinning. Her heart beat wildly. She couldn't breathe. "The train station … the fire … YOU KNEW?"

"I didn't know how … what … God help me … I should have stopped him. But I didn't until I came to see you in Seattle … saw you … saw Robyn. I returned to Paris. Demanded my father stop the man, pay him off, whatever he had to do to STOP IT!"

"AND?"

"I can't explain it, but he stood there, facing me like I'd punched him in the stomach. He placed a call. I heard him tell the person on the other end of the call to stop IMMEDIATELY."

"My God, Maxime, I could have been killed. Robyn. There would have been no Robyn. How can you stand there so calmly and tell me this. That your father tried to murder me?"

"I didn't want to tell you. You'd never have known. But I couldn't stand to carry this monstrous secret any longer. I had to tell you before you left. Gillianne, I beg your forgiveness … someway … somehow to please find it in your heart to forgive me."

Gilly collapsed on the bench, her fingers gripping the edge, looking down at the blades of grass mixed with leaves signaling that fall was coming. A few minutes ago she was enjoying an Indian summer. Now, she felt the chill of winter.

"Maxime, it seems we both made mistakes, big ones," she said looking up at him. He was now sitting beside her, elbows on his knees, fingers in a prayerful position as he scanned the moonlit sky. She took a deep breath, looked to the star-studded sky, a vision of Gramps passing through her mind. "But, here we are, tonight, together, with the product of whatever we felt for each other sleeping peacefully in your home. So, whatever sins we committed I guess God has forgiven us with the gift of a beautiful baby girl. I'm sure Gramps would say that if we have God's forgiveness can we give any less?"

Did he hear her right? He was afraid to move. He didn't deserve this beautiful woman, a woman he so very much wanted to hold in his arms to tell her he loved her. He reached for her hand, raised it to his lips, and then his forehead.

Not letting go of her hand, turned to face her.

"I can't let you leave me tomorrow without your knowing what is in my heart. My fervent prayer is that you and Robyn will return to Paris, to me, and that you will become my wife. I've tried to show you that I'm not a love-crazed Frenchman trying to take advantage of you. I brought you to the home where I grew up, introduced you to my mother," he shook his head. "And introduced you to my father. Introduced you to people who knew me as little boy growing up in this village."

Gilly raised her hand to stop him from saying any more.

"No, no. Let me finish. After I saw you in your shop ... not only had you given birth to our baby, but you had given birth to your other passion—fashion design. The fashion business. When I returned from Seattle, I began walking the streets in the fashion district. I'd look at shop windows and think how much better your designs would look in that window. A shop would be vacated and I'd go in to inquire about the rent, the space. What I'm trying to say is, you belong in Paris, you have so much to contribute, and I want you by my side as I will always be at your side. No, no. That's not quite what I'm trying to say."

He looked into her eyes. "I love you, Gillianne. My dream is that we will live out our lives together as husband and wife, supporting each other's work, loving each other, and, hopefully, having another baby. Don't answer now. All I ask is that you think about everything I've said tonight. I'll ask you after you're back in Seattle, after you have time to think about these last few days, if you will say yes to my proposal. And, I'll keep asking until you tell me to stop."

Gilly didn't respond. She stood and started walking back along the rose-bordered path to the car.

Chapter 41

Maxime parked the car in front of the house. It was dark except for a glow from the living room and hall. The front porch light was left on for them. They entered the living room, warm and cozy with a low fire. Blackie sat next to the fireplace, Maddy on stool beside him. He looked frail, almost consumed by the chair.

Maddy didn't stand to greet the couple, her face troubled, anxious as she laid her hand on her husband's arm. There was balloon of brandy untouched on the table beside his chair.

"He wouldn't go to bed. I know he isn't feeling well, Maxime, but he said he had to talk to Gillianne. I begged him to go to bed but he wouldn't. I don't know what's bothering him."

"Did you tell her?" Blackie asked, the gravely words catching in his throat as he lifted his head to look at his son.

Maxime nodded.

Blackie's eyes sought Gilly's.

"Gillianne, when I saw Robyn ... for the first time ... some six days ago, I knew I had done ... a terrible thing."

Blackie's chest began to rise and fall as he sucked in air. "I took a good look ... at myself, ... what a mean, conniving ... do anything to get what I wanted bastard. I can ... only thank the good Lord ... that I didn't succeed. I don't know why ... you would ever forgive me, but, child, ... I'm asking for your forgiveness."

Tears slowly built in his eyes, then flowed down his cheeks. He made no move to stop them. His head bent forward slightly, he gripped his chest, but never took his eyes from her.

Gilly ran to him, knelt down, grasped his hands. "Yes, Blackie, I forgive you. You were only trying to help your son. It was wrong, but I'm still here. Your granddaughter is sleeping upstairs."

His face turned pale as his blood seemed to drain away, his body withering under the weight of his guilt. Maddy ran to the phone, calling his doctor in the village to come quickly, she believed Blackie was having a heart attack.

Gilly carefully pulled Blackie's head down between his knees, began rubbing his back, chanting, "I forgive you, Blackie. Do you hear me? I forgive you."

Blackie's head bobbed that he had heard.

Maddy ran in with a towel soaked in cold water, held it to her husband's forehead and neck.

Maxime saw headlights entering the driveway and rushed to the door to let the doctor in.

Maxime and the doctor helped Blackie to the floor, and the doctor slipped a pill under Blackie's tongue. Within seconds his erratic breathing began to slow. A little color returned to his face.

Gilly squatted next to him Indian style holding his hand.

Maddy collapsed in a chair as the doctor talked softly to Blackie.

"Gave us a scare there old man," the doctor said with a chuckle. "Think you can make it to the bedroom if Maxime and I hold you up?"

"Yes ... I can make it ... and don't look so pleased ... with yourself. Just give me ... a few of those ... magic pills."

"Nitro, my friend. I told you six months ago that your heart had developed an uneven beat. Now, I want you to carry one of these capsules in your wallet, or better yet on a chain around your neck. And, take it easy for a few days. No riding that stallion of yours. Do you hear me?"

"Yes ... I hear you. I just ... had to set something straight ... with Gillianne ... before ... she leaves us tomorrow."

"Well, Maddy, keep this guy down if you can. You heard what I said to him."

"Yes, Doctor, and thank you for coming so quickly."

"No thanks required. This guy and I've been friends since we were knee high and I'm not about to let him get away from me that easy. Now, Maxime, let's you and I get your father into bed."

Chapter 42

Seattle

The jumbo jet gained speed, lifted off the tarmac, and climbed into the sky. As it banked to the left Gilly gazed out the window at the breathtaking view of the beautiful city laying beneath her. Paris. Soon the blue-gray water of the Atlantic Ocean was all she could see.

Laying her head back against the seat, her left hand relaxed on the armrest, she felt her baby grip her finger. Glancing down at Robyn kicking her legs up and down in the carrier strapped to the seat, she'll be crawling soon, Gilly thought, smiling at the little tot. She almost had the hang of it playing on the grass at the Beaumont's country villa.

At the festival Robyn didn't know what to make of the other babies, toddlers, or little people in general. But adults, oh boy, hang on to your heart because she'd snatch it away with her dark eyes, little pink lips, and red curls. Gilly wasn't sure what grabbed people first—the big dark eyes or the red curls, or maybe it was her pouty lips drawn into a smile with a giggle.

Her thoughts wandered to the scare the night before—Blackie apparently thwarting a heart attack. She hadn't talked to Gabby or Maria since she landed in Paris other than to let them know she had arrived. Had more orders come in? Was Skip still on track with his training schedule for the marathon?

But the thoughts that she kept trying to push aside kept creeping in. Gilly knew that she was facing diverging paths. Seattle. Paris. Two very different directions, each leading to a different life. Not that she couldn't reverse course if one or the other didn't work out, but she knew that whatever choice she made would be the one to shape the rest of her life. Of Robyn's life. She was anxious to see Gramps. Tell him about Maddy and Blackie—Blackie's plea for forgiveness. And, of course, Maxime's confession and proposal.

The trip was long—one stop at JFK Airport, going through customs, showing Robyn's passport that Maxime had somehow arranged cutting through red tape, and then two hours later boarding for the last leg of her return journey to Seattle. Gilly dozed much of the time always resting her hand on Robyn's arm, reassured with the feel of her soft baby skin that she was still there.

At last the flight attendants were walking the aisle checking that the seatbacks were in the upright position, tray tables stowed for landing.

Gilly caught sight of Nicole first standing at the bottom of the escalator on the baggage claim level, bobbing up and down, waving frantically to get her attention. Then Gabby, Maria, Hawk, and her mom and dad. Arthur and Cindy stood to the side. Her father relieved her of the heavy carrier, excitement in Robyn's wide eyes because all the adults around her were excited. She batted the mouse standing on the suction cup attached to the carrier between her legs as everyone cooed at her, touched her curls, thankful that she was home. Thankful that she was safe.

Anne gave her daughter a quick hug saying that Gramps was waiting back in Hansville to see her tomorrow, Saturday.

Circled by family and friends, Gilly sighed. It felt good to be home.

Chapter 43

Hansville

October, a new month, dawned with a decided chill in the air. Gilly felt invigorated, excited, and happy as she turned down the driveway and parked. Gramps was out the patio door like a shot followed by Agatha scampering to keep up. Coco squirted around, darting through her cat door into the guesthouse.

Gilly jumped out of the car and was instantly wrapped against her grandfather's big frame. He kissed her cheek and immediately let go turning to the car. Robyn was wailing—she wanted in on the action. Gilly, laughing, released the seatbelt from the carrier and hauled it out so Gramps could touch his little curly-haired great granddaughter smiling through teary eyes.

Agatha bumped down the steps leading the way to the patio door, her stub of a tail switching back and forth waiting to be let in.

"Gramps, put that teakettle on. I'm ready for one of your steamy cups of tea. Just give me a couple of minutes to put Robyn in her crib. She's more than ready for a nap."

"Two teas coming up. Skip's out on his long run—sixteen miles today. Did you pass him?"

"No. When did he start?"

"Over an hour ago. He won't be back for awhile. Must have ducked into a store. He said he had to pick up another Gatorade."

Gilly ambled into the kitchen, flopped in a chair at the table, and gazed at the sparkling waters of Puget Sound.

Home!

Gramps poured the boiling water over the teabags. "Robyn looks none the worse for wear considering her ordeal."

"Are you kidding? She was treated like royalty. Literally."

"Tell me about the Beaumonts. What were they like?"

Taking a mug from Gramp's hand, Gilly took a tentative sip of tea so as not to burn her tongue. "Gramps, they were wonderful. Maxime's mother, Madeleine … she insisted I call her Maddy … we hit it off right from the beginning. She's a wonderful, warm woman. Very caring. Nothing like what I expected from a Countess."

"Countess?"

"Yup. Count and Countess Beaumont. Pretty impressive, huh? That's what I meant when I said Robyn was treated like royalty. A little princess."

"What was he like, the Count?"

Gilly shook her head. "He seemed to change before my eyes. You'll never believe the story Maxime told me. I shudder when I think about it—the Count put out a contract to have me murdered."

Gramps mug slammed to the table, sloshing tea on his red suspenders, khaki shirt and trousers. Gilly hopped it, grabbed a kitchen towel and mopped up the table.

"Lordy, Gilly. He must have been joking."

"Hardly a joke, Gramps. It all started with Spiky. When he blackmailed Maxime … well, that's how they found out I was pregnant and then the Count feared if the media got hold of the story Maxime would lose the election for the Senate seat, something the Count had groomed—

"Hold on, sweetie. Take a breath. You mean, he thought if you were out of the picture—

"That's right. And then, all along, Bernadette, Maxime's wife … ex-wife … thought if she delivered Robyn to the Beaumonts they would take her back into the family—

"Wait, wait, wait. You said they were wonderful. How could you stay—

"Oh, Gramps, Maddy knew nothing about me or Robyn at that time, not until after Maxime returned from his first trip to see me in Seattle. Gramps, Blackie—

"Who's Blackie?"

"Maxime's father, the Count. That's what Maddy calls him. He's so filled with guilt and remorse that it's eating him alive. Gramps he's skin and bones … withering away. The night before I left he suffered a heart attack. The doctor came just in time. Gramps, Blackie was begging me for forgiveness as he clutched at his chest. His face, his body was contorted in pain as he begged me."

"Oh, child," Gramps whispered. "Did you—

"Yes, I did. How could I not. He was trying to help his son and the guilt was killing him."

"What about Maxime. Did he know what his father had done?"

Gilly left the table, wrapped the wet towel on the knob on the cupboard door. Returning to her grandfather, she looked into his eyes, shaking her head. "Yes. After he saw me and Robyn he demanded his father stop whatever he had put in action to hurt me. Gramps, he's torn with guilt like his father. He, too begged me to forgive him—for turning me away in Paris and then for not stopping his father sooner. Oh, Gramps. I don't know what to do?"

"Did you forgive him, too," Gramps whispered, his eyes riveted on Gilly's.

"I did, and then he told me of his dreams."

"Dreams?"

"That Robyn and I would return to Paris. That he and I would marry, be a family."

"My God, child, what did you say?"

"I didn't say anything. He's waiting for my answer."

"What about Skip? I thought—

"I know. Everyone thinks that Skip and I … Gramps, help me."

He slowly shook his head, put the teakettle back on the burner and stood staring at the stove. When the kettle whistled he topped off their tea, set the kettle back on the stove and returned to sit beside his granddaughter. As the steam rose from the teacup fogging his glasses, Gramps waited then wiped the mist away, and continued to look into the tea.

"As I see it, sweetie, you have two passions inside you. A creative passion for design. A passion you were born with. For most of your years, this creative passion, displayed through your designs, has been your driving force." Pausing, he peered into the green eyes looking back at him searching for understanding, searching for his wisdom, searching for answers.

"This passion to create is driving you higher and higher into the business of fashion. Will it take you to the top? I see nothing to stop you. And, this passion of yours to create will continue to drive you no matter where you live. In fact, in time you may become known worldwide."

Gramps took a sip of his tea, looked out the window as a seagull glided by on the wind. He turned back, looking at Gilly hanging on his words. He put his leathered hand on hers. "But there is this other passion that all of us are born with—the passions of the heart. Now that's a different kettle of fish. That passion searches for someone, sometimes consumed by another, always seeking someone to return the passion in kind—stronger for some than others. Do you remember what I told you when you first came to me … told me you were pregnant, and I told you that matters of the heart are complex. Your moral compass—what's right or wrong—sometimes becomes overwhelmed by emotions, passions that engulf your body?"

"Yes, I remember."

"Well, time can have a way of clearing away the fog that emotions boil up. What seemed wrong back then may, in hindsight, have not been so wrong after all."

Gilly stood, stepped to her grandfather and sat on his lap as she had when she was a little girl and he had kissed a cut on her elbow to make it better.

"I love you Gramps. Thank you."

Agatha, sleeping in her favorite spot—head in the kitchen, back half in the living room, suddenly jumped up and ran to the patio door.

"Skip must be back. He usually showers in the guesthouse and then joins me. Your car's parked in the driveway so he knows you're here. I'll put on another kettle of water. Anne brought over a fish salad yesterday on her way to the airport to meet your plane. She and your dad will be here soon."

"I'll check the mailbox for you, pick a pint of berries for Skip," Gilly said giving Gramps a kiss on his forehead. She let Agatha out the patio door and the two ambled up to the mailbox at the end of the driveway.

Skip emerged from the guesthouse and Agatha scampered up to him, jumping and whining as if they had been separated for years. He looked around for Gilly, spotted her up in the raspberry patch and trotted up to join her. He gave her a hug twirling her around and set her back on her feet squealing that she was spilling the berries.

Stepping back, he grinned. "It's good to have you back. Is Robyn with you?"

"Always," she laughed.

"Well, let's go see her."

He ran ahead to give Agatha's little legs a work out. "Gramps," he called out. You'll never guess who I found in the berry patch."

Strolling into the kitchen he found Gramps lying on the floor by the stove, the kettle whistling.

"Gilly," he yelled. "Gilly."

Hearing the tone of his yell, Gilly ran through the patio to the kitchen.

"Gramps," she screamed. His lifeless face stared up at her. "Gramps, no, no. Don't leave me. Gramps … no." She lifted his head onto her lap, holding him close, rocking back and forth. "No, Gramps … not now."

Skip hung up the receiver after giving the address to the 911 operator. He looked down at a woman whose heart was breaking and there was nothing that he, the medics, or anyone else could do to ease her pain.

Gramps was dead.

Chapter 44

"Maxime?" Gilly whispered into the phone.
"Gillianne, you're crying. What's wrong?"
...
"Gillianne, tell me."
"Gramps is dead."
"Oh, my love," he whispered. "What happened?"
"His heart ... his big heart ... it stopped. What ... I can't ..."
"Yes, you can, my darling. Same as my mother—
"What?"
...
"Blackie ... Blackie died ... last night."
"No. No. Maxime ... Maddy ...tell her I love her."
...
"I will."
"Maxime, ... I'm so sorry."
"... and I for you, my darling."
"Bye," she whispered.
"Bye," he whispered in return.
...
...
"Gillianne?"
"Yes, I'm still here."
"How is Robyn?"

"Fine. It's just … well …we're all so sad. And now, you and Maddy …"

"We must be strong," he whispered.

…

"Yes. Bye."

Bye."

…

…

Click.

Chapter 45

Dazed, the Wilder family performed the tasks that needed to be done following Gramp's death, following his wishes. He was cremated and two days later the family arranged for a quiet memorial service at the little church on the hill in Port Gamble.

Friends and family attended. All of Gilly's staff was there including Hawk and Arthur's wife Cindy. Philip Wellington, Detective DuBois and Skip arrived together.

Stacy Sinclair and her husband had just returned from Hawaii. Hearing the news they came to support Gilly. Helen Churchill and her husband made a surprise appearance. They sat in row fourteen of the fifteen rows of pews.

The service was short. The minister summed up his remarks saying that Clay Wilder was a stalwart member of the community, loved and respected by all who knew him. Will gave the eulogy, talking about his loving father and how much he adored his granddaughter and great granddaughter. The organist accompanied a trio from the church choir who sang the hymn, *Amazing Grace*. The minister closed with a prayer.

That was it? Gilly thought. Gramps was so much more. It didn't seem right. A man's life summed up in so few words.

The mourners filed into the assembly hall for refreshments provided by the Port Gamble Tea Room. Conversation was quiet, hushed, as they shared experiences and memories of Clay Wilder and his wife Betty. Gilly saw the Churchill's leaving through the front door. It was nice that they at least made an appearance, she thought. She didn't feel she had the strength to rush after them, to talk to them. But she did, thanking them for coming, hoping all was well with them. They did not respond. Turned away, walked down the small hill to the street, climbed into their car and drove away.

Those from across the sound left for the five o'clock ferry to Seattle and the Wilder's drove to Hansville. They settled in the kitchen—the enormity of the empty chair at the head of the table hitting them hard.

Gilly reached for the teakettle, stroked the handle, gulped for air and turned on the burner. No one seemed to know what to say. So, Gilly filled the kettle put it on the glowing burner and looked ahead to Saturday.

"Mom, I hope you don't mind. Skip asked if it was all right if he and Agatha came over for his Saturday training run. He has another month before the marathon. I told him I was sure you wouldn't mind."

"That's good, dear," she said with a small sigh. "Will you be coming on Saturday … as usual?"

"Yes, I want him to know I still support what he's doing." *Doing*, she thought. His goal was to finish the marathon and then to ask her what she wanted *to do* with her future. Was there a *we* in their future?

The next morning, at high tide, Will held Anne's hand as they navigated the rickety stairs to the deck below, the Queen Betty, then down the ladder to the beach. Gilly handed the two urns to her father—Grandma Betty's ashes, and Gramp's—then handed Robyn down to Anne's open arms, and then she climbed down the ladder to join them on the beach.

The day was sunny and warm for late October. It was peaceful. The only sound was the soft rhythmic waves lapping at the pilings of Queen Betty's deck and the squawk of an occasional seagull looking to plunge into the icy waters for a fish breakfast.

Will unscrewed the cap of Grandma Betty's urn and released her ashes into the soft breeze swirling out over the water. Will picked up Gramp's urn and handed it to Gilly. Closing her eyes she thanked him for his words of comfort and wisdom less than thirty minutes before he died. Opening her eyes, she released his ashes.

A whoosh of wind grasped the ashes and swept them higher and higher into the air, farther and farther out over the water. Gilly lifted Robyn from her mother's arms and pointed her finger up in the sky. The infant was mesmerized by a seagull floating on the whoosh of air.

She patted Gilly's cheek, then pointed up pushing her mother's chin up to see the bird. Suddenly another seagull joined the first, climbing higher and higher ... out of sight.

Gilly hugged her baby watching as Gramps was once again united with his beloved wife.

Chapter 46

Seattle

The ferry jostled against the pilings as it pulled into Pier 52. It was Gilly's first day back to the shop, the day after releasing Gramp's ashes. Her car bumped off the ramp and she fell into line waiting her turn at the stoplight. Parking in the back of her building, she hesitated then walked around to the front. Standing on the sidewalk in front of the shop that bore her name, she gazed at the window displays.

Somehow it looked different.

Maybe I'm different, she thought.

She had never experienced grief before, the loss of someone close. She had been scared when she found out she was pregnant. Scared seeing the flames of the fire—the fire that gutted her shop, studio, and loft where she, Nicole, and Gabby lived. The space Robyn first came to know as home. She had experienced excruciating fright when Robyn was kidnapped. But this feeling of loss was new, raw, shutting down her spirit.

Pushing against the plate-glass door she entered her shop which normally brought a smile to her face, a spring to her step at the beauty of the gleaming glass display cases, numerous mirrors giving the illusion of a large space, yet the indirect lighting providing a cozy, intimate feeling, clients feeling that the designs were made for them and them alone.

The sales girl smiled, said hello as Gilly passed. Gilly nodded and continued to the stairs leading to the loft—her apartment and design studio. Gabby called out to her, she waved and climbed the stairs. Entering her apartment she paused, looked around—everything was the same as last weekend except for the flowers. There were several bouquets, people offering sympathy she supposed. Nicole and Gabby had broken the arrangements into smaller bouquets so they didn't look like they had come from a funeral. She felt tears burning her eyes and quickly looked away.

Her design studio, her haven, her escape, was also as she had left it last weekend. Thankfully there were no flowers. Dropping her tote on a chair, she walked to the gallery board—her designs for the spring collection were in a long row. She saw a flaw in the draping of the sleeveless dress. Scrutinizing the drawing, she saw how she could remedy the error and quickly retrieved her electronic tablet from her tote. It was a spark inside her, not a shock, but a spark nonetheless and she recognized the faint surge of her blood—what was it Gramps had said, that she had a creative passion inside her for design.

Nicole burst through the door, stopped, not sure what to do, what to say. Gilly opened her arms to her vivacious friend and Nicole responded, the two hugging, rocking side to side.

It felt good to be back.

Gabby stepped through the door. "Okay, it's my turn," she said trading places with Nicole.

"Well, it's about time, girl friend," Maria called from the doorway, setting down steaming cups of coffee from the deli down the street. She gave Gilly a quick squeeze, not daring to linger for fear they'd all start crying.

Today was to be a celebration.

The boss was back.

Conversation started slowly. Arthur came in, picked up his coffee. "Good to see you, Gilly. I have some numbers to show you when you have a minute." He smiled and left. Arthur, the accountant. Who would have thought he knew that talking about the numbers showed more compassion than a funeral bouquet or even a card.

The chatter picked up steam and with the snap of the finger they were in animated discussions about the spring collection, LA Fashion week, the buyers, orders, marketing status. At one point, Gilly raced into the apartment retrieving a small bouquet of daisies. She placed them on one end of the table. She smiled at the alarmed looked on the girls' faces. Nicole had shown the card to Gabby when the bouquet arrived the day before. The flowers were from Maddy. The only words: "Thinking about you."

"Don't worry, just thought we needed to bring in a little sunshine. Did you know that a daisy never dies? It opens and closes with the sun," she said smiling. "Now, about what to include in your lookbook, Maria …"

The days passed as Gilly picked up the pieces of her life. The girls noticed, however, that one hour she was up the next down. One hour she was engaged throwing out assignments, the next she was withdrawn, staring at her tablet, stylus relaxed in her fingers instead of sketching—stroking lines, picking up colors offered on the software's color palette.

On Friday night, Maria went home. Nicole and Gabby retired to their bedrooms.

All were exhausted.

◇

The stars twinkled in the night sky. It was nine o'clock. Robyn was nestled in her crib. The apartment was still. An occasional siren, a car honking, street sounds could be heard. Gilly looked at her cell phone lying on her bedside table. She saw it vibrate—6 a.m. in Paris. If Maxime called, it was usually about this time of night. They would only speak briefly. Swap snippets of their day, always a little about Robyn, and then he'd wish her a good night's sleep.

Gilly sent Gabby and Maria to scout out the October LA fashion show with strict instructions to check in on Sheridan. Gabby called on their first night with her report. Sheridan and partner Zak had vacated their orange stucco studio. The tenant next door said they left in a hurry one night. Poof, they were gone—no forwarding address. Stiffed the neighbor for fifty dollars to pay the light bill, promising to pay the money back the next day. He never saw them again.

Gabby and Maria returned two days later full of marketing, sales, and promotion ideas they could offer at the March show.

And so the last two weeks of October went, long days at first, Gramps never far from her thoughts. Then the tempo began to pick up.

Every three nights or so, there was a nine o'clock call from Maxime. Every five or so days a package arrived for Robyn—clothes, or a stuffed animal, or some new toy on the market guaranteed to captivate an infant.

Saturdays marked the end or the beginning of the week depending on how you looked at it. They were spent in Hansville. Gilly at first returned to Seattle with Robyn after Skip's run and lunch, but then she started to spend the night, Anne loving the unexpected new routine. She had more time with Robyn as Gilly worked on the fall collection for the March show in Los Angeles. Skip spent Sunday in Gramp's den. He had a fresh angle on a new novel.

Anne prepared an early Sunday dinner while Will bundled Robyn up, taking her for a walk perched on his shoulders. Skip and Gilly, with Robyn, drove to the ferry after Sunday dinner meeting in the passenger lounge for coffee, and then bumping off the ferry's ramp they went their separate ways, rested for Monday morning.

Suddenly another week had passed. Gilly flipped the page of the calendar and stared at November, the rows of squares making up the weeks.

Saturday morning again.

Gilly packed her rolling suitcase and a gym bag with Robyn's paraphernalia. She called out to Nicole that she was leaving and would be back after Sunday dinner.

Chapter 47

Focus. Focus. Focus.

In. In.
Out. Out.
Skip's feet slapped the pavement.
"I feel good. I feel powerful. I'm a marathoner," he shouted to Bossy. She was now his pet cow, always there, every Saturday, mile five. He laughed. Bossy was in his first mental tape. When he was heading for the finish line he would run his tape over and over in his mind. Bossy and five, four, three, two, one, FINISH!

He smiled, waved, as the motorcycle pair shot passed him.
Pulled out the Gatorade, downed half, capped, back into his pack.
In. In.
Out. Out.
I can do this, he thought. Eighteen today. Thirty-six for the week.
In. In.
Out. Out.
Last long run. Final two weeks, cut the Saturday run in half. Nine miles. Hell, that'll be easy. Then coach says let the body taper off, store up energy for the big one, the big day, the marathon. Running then takes a back seat to my nutrition—lots of carbs, fluids, and the mental stuff—training tapes. He laughed. Coach says to fine-tune my engine, fill my gas tank, excite my brain. He laughed. My brain is excited—Gilly will be waiting.

In. In.

Out. Out.

Turning down the driveway, Skip spotted Gilly's car. His shirt was soaked from perspiration as he strolled into the kitchen to see who was around. Will was in the living room reading the newspaper, Anne lying on the couch catching a nap before the afternoon wave of activity. Will glanced up, whispered, "Gilly's in the guesthouse, Robyn's asleep. Why don't you take a shower down here?"

After freshening up, Skip sauntered up to the guesthouse with Agatha, rapped on the door and went inside. Gilly set down her tablet and smiled. Coco sat at the end of the table.

"How'd the run go?" she asked leaning back in her chair.

"I think I'm ready. Ready for the big day ... 26.2 miles," he said with an easy smile flopping down in the green garden chair giving Coco a few strokes down her back.

"Are you drinking coffee these days or is it off the training diet?"

"Cut back, but not off." He rose, helped himself nodding to her with the pot in his hand. She declined. "How was the fashion business this week?"

"Um. Okay, I guess. Some good, some okay, nothing bad. Skip, you haven't introduced me to your parents. Is there some reason—

"No reason, I didn't think, well, it didn't feel ... I'd like you to meet them. I've talked a lot about you. Mom's asked. How about dinner ... out ... next week?"

He frowned hearing his boss's ringtone. He stuck his fist into his pocket and put the phone to his ear. He didn't appreciate the intrusion.

Gilly watched him as spoke one word answers to whoever was on the other end of the line.

"Damn. That was my editor," he said jamming his phone back into his pocket. "I have to go. There's been a murder at a liquor store, and they want me on it right away." He stomped around the small space. "Which, of course, means I have to get going ... with the ferry, I can't get there for over an hour. Sorry. I had hoped we could spend some time together. Apologize to your mom."

Gilly stood. "I will. Don't forget about dinner with your parents next week."

"I won't," he stepped to her, held her face in his hands and gave her lips a quick peck. He held the gaze with her eyes for a brief second and then turned to leave. As he bolted through the door, Agatha on his heels, he called over his shoulder that he'd be in touch.

Gilly watched the black Jeep race down the road and then decided to check the mailbox before letting her mom know there would be one less for lunch. She found two greeting-card size envelopes. She recognized the handwriting on one, addressed to Anne and Will Wilder, without looking at the return address. Maxime. The second card was addressed to Mr. and Mrs. William Wilder, the handwriting a little shaky. The return address: Madeleine Beaumont. She surmised that they both carried messages of condolence.

Gilly's eyes glazed as she pictured Maddy, in front of the barn, paintbrush in her hand, the bouquet of flowers in the cobalt blue vase sitting on the white lace doily beside her easel.

Chapter 48

Seattle

Marathon day!

Tossing and turning, Skip finally gave up, swung his legs off the bed, and performed his stretching routine. Walking to the kitchen, he did a few head rolls, snatched a bottle of water from the refrigerator and began the hydration of his body. Drinking from the bottle, he lowered his head to see Agatha sitting patiently by her food bowl. Skip squatted and scratched her ears. "Okay, Aggie. Food then out to do your business, but that's it. Afraid you have to stay home alone today."

His pooch taken care of, Skip returned to the bedroom to put on his running clothes. When he registered he received a long-sleeved shirt made of a special material that wicks away moisture and keeps runners at a comfortable temperature. He learned the hard way to avoid cotton at all cost. At the time he registered, feeling confident, he pre-ordered a Finisher shirt.

He pulled on his light-weight pants over his running shorts. The pants could be tied around his waist along with the windbreaker if he got too hot. He looked over his list once again. There was one last item to attend to.

Picking up the little black-velvet box in his dresser drawer, he removed the diamond ring and slipped it into his trouser pocket pushing the Velcro tab down. Not only was he going to finish the marathon but he was going to ask Gilly to marry him.

Turning on the television for one last check of the weather, he heard that today luck was with the runners—forty-eight degrees now and the expected high was in the upper fifties, overcast with a light north-west wind. With a fist pump, he switched off the television.

Gilly told him she and the girls were going to wear red jackets over blue jeans so he could spot them. The plan was that they would meet him at the starting area. Give him a raucous send off and then, with Maria's knowledge of Seattle's back roads, avoid the roadblocks and find spots on the route that were virtually void of people. They'd keep cheering for him; hand him a bottle of Gatorade if he ran out, extra bandages, hat, whatever.

Giggling, Gilly showed him the list they had put together. In return he had given her the list of suggested cheering spots: 5th Avenue, Lake Washington Boulevard, Dexter Avenue, and Mercer Street. Of course, everyone knew about these locations so Maria's plan might work out better.

Skip was going to park at the Westin hotel. Shuttles were available to transport runners, family and friends to Seattle Center—the start area. The finish line was located on the track in Memorial Stadium.

Skip pinned his number on his chest and strapped the timing chip to his ankle. He received the timing chip when he registered and was told it had to be worn at all times during the race or his results could not be posted. Also the chip had to be exchanged in the finish area in order to receive a medal that he had finished the marathon—didn't matter his time or where he placed.

Skip had previously given the girls information on how to download a tracking tool application on their cell phones. All they had to do was enter the race year, event, last name, and city of the runner. The chip also made it possible for the girls' to check his progress minute-by-minute. Not wearing the chip would result in missing split times, which could result in disqualification. Each mile was to be clearly labeled on the race course and split times called at each marker.

Water and Aid stations were set up approximately every two miles providing the runners with the fluid of their choice such as Gatorade, plain bottled water, or other sports drink, in addition to basic medical items and Honey Bucket portable toilets.

Skip checked the route map one more time. The map also gave the various times when sections would be open to traffic which started at

2:15 p.m. Road blocks allowed for a seven-hour Marathon Walk finish and a six-hour Marathon Run finish. Additionally, all marathon participants still on the I-90 floating bridge after 11:00 a.m. were to be bused to the end of the bridge and allowed to finish the marathon. The race officials felt this allowed for a 25 minute-per-mile pace for walkers and an 18 minute-per-mile pace for runners. Skip's long training runs were in the eight to nine minutes-per-mile pace. If all went well, he thought he could finish in under four hours.

Skip gave Agatha a pat on her silky head and left his condo.

Skip put in his earplugs blocking out the noise of the crowd. Eleven thousand runners were expected. He planned to remove the plugs once the race started. Along the course, the cheers helped to keep the runners motivated especially the last six miles. Most marathon runners agreed that the last six miles of the race was the real test, the *real* marathon. This is when fatigue really sets in and when many runners gave up.

He told Gilly he was going to start the race at the back of the pack. In college, he had started his first marathon in the front, right after the wheelchairs, and a runner had trampled on his foot. His coach told him that starting in the rear you could weave in and out as space between runners opened up plus it made you feel good to be passing others.

Wheelchair athletes were first and had an escort throughout the race. It was required that they wear hard-shell helmets and that their wheelchairs be adequately equipped for safety.

Skips eyes darted over the crowd looking for the four girls in bright red jackets. He saw Nicole first, holding a sign: *Go Skip Go!* He strolled over to them grinning as he removed the earplugs. Handing them to Gilly, she threw her arms around him and wished him well. Not wanting to miss a thing, Maria, Gabby and Nicole took their turn hugging their favorite runner.

Gilly showed him the extra Gatorade bottles she was carrying and Nicole said she had extra bandages in case of a blister.

It was nearing time for the race to start. The wheelchair athletes were already on their way. The Marathon Walk started at 7:15 a.m. The Half Marathon Run, thirteen miles, at 7:30 a.m. The Marathon Run was scheduled to start at 8:15 a.m.

Skip downed sixteen ounces of water and handed the empty bottle to Nicole. Even though he wasn't thirsty, he had to be sure he was fully hydrated. It didn't matter now but could mean later on whether he finished the race or not.

And, he was going to finish!

Chapter 49

It was time!
The moment he had trained for!
The official raised the starting gun.
Raised the microphone to his lips.
"On your mark.
"Get set.
"Go!"

Skip shifted foot-to-foot waiting for the throng of runners to move. Slowly the swarm, like a tsunami making its way to shore, began to inch forward.

He took a step. Another. He was on his way.

Skip picked his spots passing one runner at a time.

He zigged.

He zagged.

By mile four a large group of runners had dropped out. They had run the 3.1 miles of a 5K race and had had the thrill of starting a marathon. The crowd lining the course cheered their success.

Skip kept moving up.

He felt great, exhilarated but was careful to continue hydrating. Every two miles he grabbed a bottle from the outstretched hand of a volunteer at the water station.

His legs were strong, his breathing controlled.

In. In.

Out. Out.

There were spectators on the road ahead.

The Lake Washington Boulevard cheering section. Four red jackets, eight arms in the air were waving wildly at him, he waved back, fingers forming a V that he was okay.

Grasping a water bottle at the ten-mile water station he noticed the group behind him shrank. The runners had hit 10K, 6.2 miles.

In. In.

Out. Out.

Swinging around Seward Park he knew he'd passed the fourteen-mile mark. He ate his second energy bar. Picked up water at station sixteen. He began to feel the strain in his legs and slowed his pace. He hadn't seen the red jackets since Lake Washington Boulevard.

In. In.

Out. Out.

To finish in a certain time was not his goal. It didn't bother him that he had slowed his pace. The goal was to finish. He fingered the ring in his pocket, smiled, picking up his pace again. He figured he was running a nine- or ten-minute mile. As he grabbed the water at station twenty, the volunteer hollered, "Only six more."

It hit him.

The wall.

He had felt it before in college.

"Focus.

"In. In.

"Out. Out."

He slowed. Ate his last bar. Hands on hips, he walked three minutes, drank a water from a cup in the outstretched hand.

Started to run again. Easy, slow pace. He focused on the road in front of him. He didn't dare look up.

"Focus, Hunter."

In. In. Out. Out.

"You can do this, Hunter."

In. In. Out. Out.

"You've done it before. Come on, boy. Focus"

He could see Memorial Stadium. The street was lined deep. People were cheering their runner on, holding signs, yelling out names, numbers.

In. In. Out. Out.

"Focus. Half mile more. Focus."

His feet were screaming at him. He felt a cramp in his calf.

"Focus. Focus."

In ... In .... Out .... Out ...

He was in the stadium. The finish line was just on the other side.

In ... In .... Out .... Out ...

The roar was thundering.

"Just a few more feet, Hunter"

In ... In ... Out ... Out ...

Red jackets. Red jackets. Focus.

In ... In ... Out ... Out ...

Skip's feet slapped the last two steps, felt the tape on his chest. He pushed through.

He finished!

He bent over, hands on his thighs. Breathed deep. A race official walked up to him, un-strapped the chip from his ankle. "Good job, Hunter." His official time was recorded.

Nicole was the first to hug his sweat-stained shirt, then Gilly, Maria, and Gabby. Hawk thumped him on the back.

Skip reached into his pocket, felt the ring, grasped it tight in his fingers. He looked over at Gilly standing a few feet away. A man stepped to her side. Put his arm around her. Stepped back, his arm slipping off her shoulder.

Then she was walking toward him. *She's walking to me.*

Gilly hugged him. Her arms tight around him. She stepped back. "Skip, you did it. You finished. Your goal."

"Yeah." He suddenly felt weak, his body giving way to the extreme exertion. His eyes darted between Gilly and the man standing next to her ... again.

Gilly looked from the man to him. "Skip, I'd like you to meet Maxime Beaumont. Maxime meet Skip Hunter, the man we've been cheering for."

Maxime put his hand out, but Skip had no strength. His fingers released the ring in his pocket. He stood, arms hanging at his sides, staring at the man.

"Maxime, I'll meet you at the tunnel. Give me a few minutes with Skip."

Maxime nodded, squeezed her shoulder. "Nice race, Skip. Not many can accomplish what you just did." He walked up the track to the exit tunnel.

Skip looked at Gilly.

Gilly stepped closer. They were alone in the thundering crowd.

"When you began training for the marathon you told me your goal was to finish. Skip you did it. You also told me that you were using your training, and then the running of the race to move your life forward, that you would then see if I was open to move along with you. We've been through so much together … you've been there for me so many times. But you and I are going to move forward on different paths now. I'm returning to Paris with Maxime … Robyn and I—"

"Skipper, Skipper." Diane shot in front of Gilly, hugged Skip as if he was going to evaporate. "Let's go celebrate. The whole newsroom watched on television. You should have heard them screaming. I was checking your time with my cell. Didn't think I'd make it here before you left. The crowds are crazy." Diane noticed Gilly. "Ah, Gillianne Wilder. Wasn't he wonderful?"

"Yes. He's wonderful. Bye, Skip." Gilly tried to smile. She leaned around Diane, kissed his cheek. "Keep writing. I expect to see your book in print someday."

Skip watched her as she walked away from him.

He had finished the race but lost the girl.

Chapter 50

Gillianne's Paris Boutique

Paris

The brunette television reporter looked into the camera and smiled.

"Bonjour, Paris. Yesterday afternoon reporters from news outlets around the world crushed into the Carrousel du Louvre on the last day of Paris Fashion Week.

"The media and the fashion industry's elite witnessed a special moment on the runway. Gillianne Wilder, living in Paris a mere three years, revealed her new collection to a standing ovation. Following her last model down the runway with her adorable daughter, both redheads, they smiled and waved to the crowd.

"Her husband, Senator Maxime Beaumont, strode down the aisle between the spectators with a bouquet of flowers for his wife and a small nosegay for his daughter. Reaching up, he placed their three-month old son in her arms, kissed her passionately, and then kissed his daughter handing her the flowers to the roar of the crowd clamoring for more. Madame Wilder opened her first shop soon after her arrival from Seattle and continues to maintain her original shop in Seattle."

Maxime shut off the television and turned to his wife. "So, you are the talk of Paris, my darling. I knew you could do it. Your collection is beautiful ... you are beautiful," he said pulling her into his arms.

"Uh, excuse me, Senator. Your car is waiting out front."

"Thank you, Eric. And the car seats ... are they fastened securely?"

"Yes, sir."

"Wonderful. Gillianne and I will be right down with Robyn and Clayton."

With his family safely ensconced in the limousine, Maxime slipped in the other side next to his wife. He kissed her hand and then gazed out at the sparkling water of the Seine as the vehicle merged with the Paris traffic. "Mother is beside herself that we're joining her in the country with the children. She insisted that she and Gertie could handle Robyn and the baby so we could have some time alone. But, she made me promise I would see to it that you had time to rest."

He turned ... caught the sparkle in his wife's eyes, and kissed her cheek. "How lucky I am to have you by my side. I love you, Gillianne."

"I love you too, sweetheart," she said raising her lips to his. Smiling, she looked out the window at the shops, the flower stalls, and the cafes. "Oh ... Eric, can you stop a minute at that bookstore?" Grasping Maxime's hand, she smiled up at him. "Mom called this morning. She said Skip's book is in print. I want to see if they have it. I'll just be a minute. " She planted a quick kiss on Maxime's cheek and scooted into the store, pausing briefly at their window display.

"Oui, Madame, may I help you?"

"Oui, s'il vous plaît. The book in the window ... over in the corner. I'm afraid it's slipped off the holder."

The woman walked to the side of the display, reached in and picked up the book. "This one, Madame?"

"Oui, merci."

Gilly paid for the book, stood a moment running her finger over the title and the author's name: *The Seattle Gold Heist, by Skip Hunter.* She flipped through a couple of pages and found the dedication her mom had told her about.

*In memory of my friend Clay Wilder
who held the key to the mystery.*

The End

ACKNOWLEDGEMENTS

The following book was extremely enlightening as to the training required to run a marathon: David A. Whitsett, Forrest Dolgener, Tanjala Mabon Kole, *The Non-Runner's Marathon Trainer*, McGraw Hill eBook, 1998

Tasha Hériché—thanks your painstaking editing and suggestions for the *French connection*.

Roger and Pat Grady—thanks for finding the loose ends and helping to close the loops, as well as suggestions for missing backstory.

Lorna Mae Prusak, Vera Kuzmyak, and Molly Tredwell for their review of the manuscript and continued support.

Thank you all!